BOOK TWO IN THE IDEA MAN TRILOGY

I0633244

THE
MARKED
MAN

a novel

KRISTIN HELLING

THE MARKED MAN
by Kristin Helling

This is a work of fiction. Names, characters, businesses, places,
events and incidents are either the products of the author's
imagination or used in a fictitious manner. Any resemblance to
actual persons, living or dead, or actual events is purely
coincidental.

Printed in the United States of America
First Printing, 2020

ISBN-13: 978-1-946921-14-7

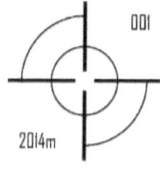

ADRENALINE

Adrenaline
An imprint of Wordwraith Books, LLC
705-B SE Melody Lane #149
Lee's Summit, MO 64063
e-mail wordwraiths@gmail.com
website www.wordwraiths.com

Edited by J. R. Frontera
Cover Design by Deranged Doctored Designs
Format Design by Rod Galindo
Proofread by Wayne Burnop

Kristin's email author@kristinhelling.com
Kristin's website kristinhelling.com

The Library of Congress Cataloging-in-Publication Data is
available upon request.

Dedication
For Austin,
Remington,
The Wordwraiths,
and Indiepub.

ALSO BY KRISTIN HELLING

Books available where all books are sold.

THE IDEA MAN TRILOGY
(comedic, suspense thriller)

The Idea Man
The Marked Man
The True Man

THE MASTERMIND MURDERERS SERIES
(psychological, crime thriller)

The Altruism Effect
The Bystander Effect
The Carbon Effect
The Domino Effect

STANDALONE SERIES
(soft sci fi Thriller)

Capsule

TABLE OF CONTENTS

ONE

Dear Noriana,

If you are reading this letter, it probably means that I am gone. I am about to embark on a task that may get me killed. This may be the last thing I ever get to say to you. Please know, my time with you was more than I could have dreamed of when I came to Paris.

When I met you, I was lost. Not just lost in the museum... I was lost in my identity. I didn't know who I was. Just a college drop-out working for a dead-end job as a delivery boy for a magazine who never wanted me as a writer. I'd watched time after time, as all the other people I graduated high school with succeeded in the job market, money market, and relationship pool. I sucked at all of those.

All I knew was that I needed a way out. An escape from the path I led. Fate brought me to that museum (or a note left by a stalker... whatever you want to call it), and to that hallway where I heard your beautiful voice, like a song I never wanted to stop listening to.

Noriana Page, I am so sorry I brought you into this mess that is my journey. I hope you can forgive me for dying before we got the chance to live our lives without fear of being followed or hunted. All I know is that I am grateful for the time I did have leading to this, because you woke me.

Parker Rubec

Dear Mom,

I'm sorry I've given you so many heart attacks since I left home. I know sometimes I can be very unpredictable and seem altogether careless about things in general. I'm sorry those unpredictable choices may not be what you dreamed for me.

If you are reading this, it's because I didn't make it. I chose to do a dangerous job in order to help with the bigger picture. I know that doesn't make much sense to you, but hopefully someday you will understand. You were a great Mom to me. I look back on my childhood with happiness, even though Stephen will always be your #1 son. Hehe.

And if you want more answers, contact Greyson Price.

4

I just wanted you to know that I love you and thank you for everything you've done for me. Tell Dad I love him, too.

Parker

TWO

Two Weeks Earlier...

From the kitchen of his studio apartment, he looked across the room at the locks of brunette hair that spilled over Noriana's shoulders. In the golden light from the large loft windows, Parker hardly concentrated on the glass in his hand. He absently pressed a lemon onto its rim.

"What?" she asked, smiling.

"I just can't believe you're here. With me. In my apartment. In Kansas City. You came all the way from Paris."

"Well, I'd rather spend Christmas break with you here than back home in San Francisco. Plus, it's only for a little while."

"I'll take what I can get." He turned to prepare the other drink, pulling a can of sparkling water from the fridge.

"So, are you going to tell me what happened after your interview in New York?" she asked from the couch. "It's not like you to just quit an entire book tour."

Man, she just gets right down to it, doesn't she? He took a deep breath, held it for a second while he debated whether to be honest with her or not, then exhaled loudly. She'd been there when he'd first met Greysen. She knew the story too, now. Of course he could be honest with her. "I don't know..." He hesitated. "I think I'm in trouble, Nori." His voice had a hint of a shake to it.

"What else is new?" she teased.

"This is real, though." He moved around the kitchen island and handed her one of the drinks, a lemon Italian soda with a wedge split on the rim of the glass.

"Tell me about it," she said softly, puckering her red lips.

"I constantly feel like the person behind me is going to put one of those rags up to my face and make me pass out like in the movies. If there is nobody in Kansas City right now after me, they will be soon. It's only a matter of time."

Noriana furrowed her brow. It appeared her kidding tone sobered from the tone in Parker's voice. She moved over on the couch.

Parker took her lead and sat down next to her. He set his Italian soda down on the coffee table. He sighed and put his hands on his knees, bracing himself. "I got a call, Nori. From a woman claiming to be Molly." The words forming on his lips felt unnatural.

Noriana placed her hand on Parker's hunched shoulder. "How can you be sure she was telling the truth, though? You told her it was fiction, right?" The inflection in her voice told him she knew the direction this conversation was headed.

"If... if Molly's alive..." He heaved a great sigh. "Greysen ultimately decided to go into hiding after he thought all hope of Molly being alive was lost. He would have never left without knowing she was safe first, you know? And she said there are people now who will never stop hunting me. I think she means Edrick and his men. Molly—this... woman—implied that because I wrote Greysen's story, the bad guys are going to think I know where he is. And they don't want me. They want *him*."

"But you *don't* know where he is."

Parker pushed back from her. "I know, right! Nobody does. Have you seen him at all while you're in Paris?"

She shook her head. "No, I haven't. Not since that last time we were outside of Rue de Saint-Germain. I always look now, of course. I always pay attention to the homeless. It's crazy how you don't notice these things when you go about your everyday life. I walk by so many people on the street... it's as if Greysen made me aware." She took a sip of her drink, which was now sweating on the outside of the glass, then set it down next to Parker's.

"But to go unnoticed was his plan. He knew that people try to avoid the eye of homeless people. So he created a character for himself where he could blend in and nobody would bother giving him a second glance. It's a perfect cover, right?"

"Maybe *you* should do that." Noriana smirked.

He chuckled, and then leaned back on the couch and composed himself. "I *could* become homeless..."

"Joke, Parker. That was a joke!" She laughed and took another sip from her drink. "But why would they come after *you*? Even if you know the entire story of what Greysen did, you didn't *do* anything but write what happened to him. You are a writer!"

Parker glanced up at his vinyl record player, staring off into space a moment before stretching his neck side to side and looking back at Noriana. "I know! But apparently because I wrote his story, they think I have a relationship with the guy. And I guess they think that means I know where he's hiding. And they want him dead. Soooo."

She heaved an audible sigh, her shoulders sinking to match his. "That's serious shit, Parker. What do you do?"

Parker shrugged and shook his head. Then splayed his hands in a helpless gesture. He was no Greysen Price. He was just a college drop-out from Kansas City who was pretty good at writing books. "What *can* I do? I probably just have to wait it out. Maybe if I just lay low long enough, they'll give up? I mean... they eventually stopped looking for Greysen, right?"

Noriana rolled her eyes. "Sure. Probably after *years*, Parker. And if Molly is calling you up, then I'd say no. They *didn't* stop looking for him."

A little twinge of dread settled in Parker's stomach. He swallowed hard. "Well... it's the best I got. I mean, if I'm not traveling all over the place showing up on tv in interviews all the time, I should be harder to find, right? I'm just a normal guy in Kansas City, now. I'll just hang out here, keep my head down, stay quiet..." He gave her a smile. "With you. What do you want to do while you're here?"

She sighed and rolled her eyes again, but seemed to accept his pitiful logic. At least for now. She took another gulp of lemon sparkling water and stood, then walked to the large, loft windows. "Be with you." She smiled and swayed her hips around to face him.

He remembered the time in the small Versailles Bed and Breakfast just then, when their relationship seemed almost completely over. Back then, just as fast as he'd met her, they were breaking up.

He stood up and joined her at the windows. Then reached out and placed his hand on her waist. She moved into his chest and he brushed her bangs away from her eyes. She wasn't much shorter than him. He tipped his head down and kissed her on the lips. It'd been way too long.

For the last several months, they'd endured a long-distance relationship. He'd been off around the nation on his book tour while she continued her studies in France.

"I'm cool with doing this all day," she joked. Then she grew more serious. "Just, honestly, let's do anything that gets your mind off all of Greysen's mess. Surely you don't have to worry about that here, anyway, in your hometown.

Let's for once have a normal time together and do normal couple things."

He smiled and pulled her closer. "I could take you to the Liberty Memorial."

She shrugged. "What's that?"

"It's a monument they built for World War I. It has great views of the city from the top of it."

"Do you have any art museums?" she asked, then twirled away from his grasp. She placed her glass on the coffee table and headed for the bathroom.

"Oh, yeah! Duh! Of course," he called out to her across the room. "We have the Nelson. I don't know why I didn't think of that first."

"As long as there are no assassins at the Nelson, I'm cool with that!" She slipped into the bathroom and shut the door.

Parker had a momentary flash of panic. And not because of the assassin comment. He tried to remember if he'd left his dirty underwear balled on the bathroom floor. Or if there were pubes on the toilet seat. Or what kinds of medicine he had in the cabinet.

He reached for his glass and gulped more water.

Well, whatever might be in there, it was too late to do anything about it now. Maybe, if she saw any such things in there, it would strengthen their relationship?

He could only hope.

Parker fetched his laptop out of the messenger bag by the door and pulled up the museum's website, mostly to keep himself from obsessing over the cleanliness of his bathroom and to kill the time before Noriana was ready to go, but also to check on the topic of the current special exhibit.

A notification pinged at the top right corner of his screen. He generally ignored those, but this one caught his eye. It was from an actual person, and not a blatant ad or promotion. He clicked on it to pull up the full email, and couldn't help his gaze jetting down to the signature line.

It's from Molly. His heart plummeted to his stomach.

The toilet flushed from behind the bathroom door.

His head shot up to the closed bathroom door, then back down to the screen. He scanned the words, one toppling over the other.

Parker,

I found your email address by contacting your publisher to ask them where I could send a piece of fan mail. You should really talk to them about handing out your personal information. As if an email is personal, but that's where it starts. I hope you believed me when I told you that if I was able to find you, then do not doubt they will find you, too. I need to keep this email short. Will you meet up with me? I am in New York, but I can fly anywhere in the nation. I must have a conversation with you. In person.

Trust,

Molly Green

The black text on the screen burned into his eyes. He rubbed at them before staring at the email once more, to see if it was real. A tiny fire burned in his stomach. *What the hell?* –was his first thought. Why was she trying to contact him again? Did she have new information? Why did she want to meet with him in person?

And his publisher was just giving out his info? He supposed that part was his fault, though. He'd given them this email address as his mode of contact for fans, after all.

Because, what fans? Who would ever contact him?

This answered that for him.

He slumped onto the couch with his laptop as Noriana came back out of the bathroom, her hair pulled into a ponytail and a fresh layer of red on her lips. She stopped short at the look of him. "What?" she asked, emotion draining from her face.

"Huh? Uhh, nothing." He scratched the back of his neck, avoiding her gaze.

"You're as white as a ghost, Parker. What happened?"

He leaned forward and put the laptop on the coffee table, then clicked back to the Nelson website. *We just talked about how we want to do normal couple things. If I tell her about this email, it will definitely derail our day.* On the other hand, maybe he should email Molly back. If she was this adamant about getting ahold of him, she must have something pressing to tell him.

Of course, he couldn't really email her back or go to meet her while Noriana was here.

"I'm, uhh, just upset that the black-and-white photography exhibit closed. They have something else now." He hoped she couldn't see right through him. He immediately felt bad for lying.

"Psh, that's no big deal. There's so much else to see. No sweat, Parker." She knelt down and shuffled in her suitcase before grabbing her purse. "You ready?"

"Yeah." Parker hesitated. He really wanted to write Molly back, get it over with so he could enjoy his day with Nori. "Gimme just a moment..." With her across the room, he pulled up Molly's email again.

"While you're finishing up, I'm going to go down and get some fresh air. Meet you down there?"

He looked up at her. "Okay! I'll be right there."

She ducked out of the apartment.

His words fled from his fingers onto the keyboard like fire:

Molly,

Fine. I'll meet. In Kansas City. I'm sick of traveling. I don't know why you want me, anyway.

P

Short. Sweet. And to the point. It was just a matter of when she would get here. Parker wanted to run down the stairs, out onto the street to Nori, and tell her what had just happened.

17

But he couldn't ruin what they had going now.

He couldn't help but think of how his entire life would be so different if he hadn't been at Gare du Nord in Paris that day, which felt like forever ago. He never would have met Greysen. He never would have been wrapped up in all the deadly drama between Greysen and the men who hunted him.

But he also never would have met the girl who waited for him outside. And he'd go through all of that drama and terror again if it meant he'd get to be with her. Paranoia or not, he couldn't screw this up.

THREE

T he Nelson had been a good choice for their outing; a hidden gem in the middle of the city. It had huge pillars on the sides and in the center of the building, and posed as a frequent backdrop for wedding photo shoots. The museum overshadowed a vast front lawn of green grass spread all the way to the street, where people often had picnics and played flag football. The famous Kansas City shuttlecock sat towards the end of the lawn.

As they walked through the renaissance sculpture garden, Parker kept his eyes on Noriana. He loved seeing her in her natural element. She was far more cultured than he was. The most attractive thing to him was that she possessed a passion for this kind of stuff that could match his passion for writing. He'd dated girls in the past who'd made him feel guilty for pursuing his craft, as if he thought it was more important than their relationship. He was happy to have found somebody that could parallel his passion for something and understand.

Of course, the fact they had a long-distance relationship helped his writing as well. It allowed him plenty of time to work while he was depressed about her being across the globe. He knew she'd only be at school until May, though... unless, of course, she landed her dream job in France.

But even if she did come back to the United States after graduating from the University de Sorbonne, she lived in San Francisco. That's where her home and family was.

Family. Perhaps he should bring Noriana to meet his parents while she was here. In his adult life, he didn't spend much time with his family. They each led their own lives, and his mom was not in favor of the fact he'd suddenly come into a fortune he had a hard time explaining.

"Parker!"

He snapped out of it. Noriana was paces ahead and he rushed to catch up.

"You are always in a daze!" She shook his shoulder. "I asked you if you wanted to go to the food court and get something to eat?"

He looked at the beautiful girl in front of him. "Yeah, sure. Sorry."

She laughed. "No big deal! I'm not sure why I'm surprised. You've always been in your own world."

They walked through the grandeur hallways of the Nelson Atkins Museum of Art, headed towards the food court. Of course this museum was nothing compared to the likes of the Louvre, Musee D'Orsay, or Le Centre Pompidou. But it was one of its own. And Noriana seemed to be enjoying it. That's all that mattered.

The food court was even one to impress. Large, caramel-colored slate tiles lined the floor, and there was a beautiful fountain in the middle of a large courtyard, with a second story around the perimeter that looked down upon the people eating at the tables below.

They walked up to the assembly line of people picking up sandwiches and fruit plates. As they worked their way through, choosing what they wanted to eat, Parker kept a close eye on a man wearing a nice suit and a pearl tie. He was sitting by himself at a table. Amongst all the people enjoying their time at the museum and getting a bite to eat, he didn't seem to quite fit in. He was entirely out of place.

"You want tea or coke?" Noriana asked him.

"Err, sweet tea please." He kept his attention on the man with the pearl tie.

21

"Who are you looking at?" she asked as they reached the end of the line.

"Shh..." he said out of the corner of his mouth as he reached into his back pocket and retrieved a small, light brown, leather wallet. He paid the woman and Noriana picked up the tray of food. They wandered into the courtyard of tables.

Noriana heaved a loud sigh. "What's wrong with you? I thought we were—"

"Hold... on..." he pushed her off again. He guided them to a table on the opposite end of the courtyard and as they passed, the pearl tie man's eyes followed them down the lane.

They sat down and Parker reached across the table, grabbing Noriana's hand. "Nori... I think this guy has been following us."

"Huh?" she asked, turning her head to look.

"Well don't look!" he urged her.

She gave a stern look back at him.

"Don't make it obvious. Man. I knew they'd come for me. Whether or not I responded to the email, they were coming. They're here right now. Shit. What do I do?" He felt a tightness in his chest that gripped all the way up his esophagus.

"*What* email?"

Noriana's voice existed in the back of his mind. At the end of the tunnel. Breathing

22

became a chore. He felt like he was in one of those dreams where you lose control of one or more of your senses. Where you're trying to spot something in a crowd, but your peripheral vision starts blacking out. Or one of those dreams where you're trying to run fast but your legs just can't do it. Like you're in a pile of quick sand and can't escape.

He couldn't escape now. *We're in a public place...* He repeated it over and over in his mind. Just when he was about to implode and allow the panic attack to engulf him entirely, a woman screamed from across the courtyard. Parker's head shot up to see a woman raging at the man with the pearl-colored tie. She was causing quite the scene at his table, and Parker heard her throw around an f-bomb or two.

He looked up at Noriana with wide eyes, then shrugged. It was hard *not* to stare.

"I said, who *are* you?" The woman had an abrupt staccato on the last three words.

A man sat at a table nearby who appeared to have been with the woman.

Parker sensed the guy's hesitation as he joined the woman standing over the table.

"Are you alright miss?" The pearl tie guy asked.

"Answer me! You've been following us around for the like a week now!"

23

The woman's partner glanced over at Noriana and Parker's table.

Parker quickly looked away from the scene, trying to make it seem like he hadn't been watching, though it was obvious.

Noriana pushed her chair back and stood. "C'mon Parker, I'm over this." Without waiting for his response, she turned from the scene and hurried out of the food court.

Parker bolted after her, looking back at the table. He couldn't tear himself away from the scene, but he had to catch up with Noriana. *Do we bus our own plates?* He glanced around the food court looking for a trash but didn't see one. And all the attention was on the scene. *Awe well!* He followed after Nori. *Better them than me!* That couple also got weird vibes from the man in the suit and pearl tie. At least he had been validated in the fact that the guy was indeed, creepy. And a sensation of relief washed over him that he'd most likely had nothing to do with Greysen. But that was just it. He *most likely* wasn't following Parker. That doesn't mean he wasn't.

He caught up to Noriana.

"See? He wasn't following us," she reassured him as they walked out the side door of the Nelson and into the yard that held a large infinity pool fountain.

"We just got lucky because that other couple intervened," Parker mumbled under his breath. He shoved his hands into his pockets.

"You still think he was following you?" Nori asked, sounding annoyed. She stopped, turned to him, and crossed her arms. "He was just a creepy dude that was out of place. That other couple thought he was following them, too! Parker." She grabbed his arm and turned him. "Is my entire trip going to be us running again? I thought we talked about this. And more importantly... *what email*?"

He sighed. *She remembered.* He held the gaze of her piercing eyes.

"Parker." She reached over and grabbed both of his hands, guiding him toward the parking lot. "Do you want to tell me happened back there?" Her voice was soft, non-invasive.

"I'm sorry I didn't tell you about the email—I should have."

"Well what I'm not okay with, is the fact you majorly *freaked out* back there! I want to make sure you're okay." The scarf she held up to her chin swayed in the breeze.

"Yeah... I panicked. I don't even know." He looked down at his shoes.

"Here, get in the car. I can drive us back. It'll be okay."

Parker rounded the car to the passenger side, thoughts running like crazy in his mind. He pulled the collar of his jacket up on his neck as a chill in the air whisked by.

The chill could only remind him that the moment he let his guard down, would be the moment Molly's prophecy would come true.

FOUR

Parker turned on his side, crunching his rib against the death bar on his black futon in the darkness of his apartment.

Why do futons exist? he cursed, looking at the clock in his kitchen. *6am.* He turned his head and followed the wooden floors of his apartment up to his bed. Since it was a studio apartment, the bed was in the same room as the living room, though could be separated by a baby blue curtain if need be.

He saw Noriana's hand dangling down the side of the bed. Her breathing was deep and held a distinct pattern. She was fast asleep. After they'd left the museum, she had been beat, probably from the jet lag of flying across the world in one day, though she'd said the best option would be to stay awake as long as possible and go to sleep at a normal bed time so she could get used to his time zone. As soon as she'd hit the bed, she was out.

They'd been together for a whole year and he hadn't slept with her yet. Well they had *slept* together in the same bed, technically, in the Bed and Breakfast in Versailles, but they hadn't had sex.

It didn't help that they'd spent most of their relationship on the phone and through webcam.

Parker heaved a sigh and rolled over on the couch. Why had he even decided to come home to begin with? He could have stayed in Paris. But that would have been a great way to eat up all his money. Of course, he didn't have a job here, either, but having an apartment in Paris was double the expense to having one here in Kansas City. And he didn't want to eat through his advance too quickly, before he had another book out

And then of course there was the anxiety of never writing another good book. He heaved a loud sigh, then sat up on the couch. The blanket fell off his shoulders.

He hadn't gotten a huge pay day for writing a masterpiece. He'd gotten the publishing deal for his last book because of who it was about.

There was a big difference. And that would always weigh heavy on his mind as a writer.

At least he'd gotten the exposure. That was more than he could have ever asked for.

Except for that exposure alerted the bad guys to who I was, too, and maybe even helped them figure out where to find me. Yay for exposure! He rolled his eyes.

Who knew, maybe he'd be dead before he'd have to write his next book.

That's not even a funny joke. The hum of the heater kicked on. He sighed and reached for his smart phone. He'd never had insomnia, but when there was a lot on his mind, it was hard to get to sleep. And he was also used to talking to Noriana so late at night since their time zones were seven hours apart.

Maybe if he looked at his phone it would make his eyes drowsy. He pulled it up and turned the brightness down.

He looked at social media. Nothing of particular interest. Cat videos and pictures of a cake someone he went to high school with had posted. And babies. So many babies.

He'd watched the evolution of his social media feed throughout the years. First it had been full of photos of partying. And keg stands.

Then it was photos of weddings, so many weddings. And now babies.

Not like he hardly posted anything of his own. But it was nice to scroll through and see things his relatives were up to, or stats about the Royals.

Next, he pulled up his email. Junk mail from different websites and retailers. An email from his landlord to all tenants telling them not to park in a certain area of the lot outside while they got it resurfaced.

It's about time.

His stomach flipped as he saw the next email. He sat up. *Molly.*

"I'm here. Meet me at Opera House when they open in the morning."

That was fast. He'd just confirmed he'd meet with her yesterday. She must have hopped on the first flight. This *was* urgent. Which only made him more nervous.

He looked up at Noriana again. Perhaps he could meet with Molly, and then bring Noriana breakfast before she even knew he was gone.

He rose and quickly got ready, then slipped out the door. Opera House, a coffeehouse in the neighborhood, didn't open for another hour, but he figured he'd get there early and wait. As he hit the outside, he pulled his collar over his neck. It was cold enough that a fog escaped his nose as he breathed, visible in the air. He passed by a dog park, and a woman doing yoga while her Yorkie peed on all the bushes in proximity to her.

Everyone that was awake at that time was just going about their business, like nothing else in the world was happening. As if he wasn't in danger. As if it didn't even matter that right now, he felt like he was walking to his doom. He had no idea why Molly wanted to meet, or what she wanted with him, but his imagination was sure running wild with the possibilities... most of them terrible.

He walked to Opera House, a corner shop that served multiple purposes. It was a coffeehouse, a sit-down restaurant, and a bar. The décor was industrial: all concrete and raw-looking, with metal trimmings.

After pacing for a good while, he waited until the lights were on and the opening employees were settled before he went inside. He walked up to the grill counter to order his biscuits and gravy before choosing a high-top table with barstools to climb onto. He figured right before he left to go back home, he would grab Noriana a coffee and scone.

Nobody else was there yet who looked like they could be the woman he was supposed to meet. He fidgeted on the stool and watched out the large windows to try and catch a glimpse of her before she saw him.

A large man with a beard and 2-inch gaged ears brought out his small tray of biscuits with delicious sausage gravy slopped all over it.

"Thanks, man." Parker nodded to him and took the tray, sliding it onto the table in front of him. His eyes kept darting anxiously toward the many doors—why did this place have so many doors, anyway?—as he forked up some of the flaky biscuit and shoved it into his mouth.

Just as he swallowed, his stomach lurched up into his throat and he cupped a napkin to his mouth as a woman walked towards him. She wore skinny jeans and a navy-blue jacket. Tight black ringlets of hair hung to her chin, and her complexion was smooth and flawless. Even though he knew she must be Greysen's age, age looked good on her.

With confidence, she placed her to-go coffee cup on his table.

He chased another piece of biscuit with a small chunk of sausage around his plate as she sat across from him, her face serious. *How does she even know it's me?* "You're..." He cleared his throat, stretching his neck back and forth. "I didn't realize you were black." He immediately regretted speaking. *I'm such an idiot!* He punished himself inside his mind.

She choked on a sip of coffee she had taken before setting the cup down. "That's rude," she answered sternly, not even a hint of a smile on her lips.

Shit! Parker... what the hell. What are you thinking? You weren't *thinking.* He just hadn't been prepared to meet up with such an attractive woman. His tendency to stick his foot in his mouth had struck again. "I didn't mean to be rude," he said quickly, trying to backpedal. "You just aren't the person I was expecting." She was supposed to be some lady around his parents age that had let herself go. She was definitely out of Greysen's league. At least the Greysen he knew. Or thought he knew. "But... you're Molly?"

She nodded. "I... I planned out what I was going to say to you, Parker, but now I just don't know." She looked down at her lap, a sadness overcoming her eyes. "How did you meet my Greysen?" she asked at last. "Let's start there."

Parker thought about it a minute. He leaned forward over the table, over his plate of biscuits and gravy. "How do I know I can trust you?" he hissed. "This is nuts! You tracked me down and flew all the way to KC overnight to talk to me, just to ask me how I met him? Why couldn't you ask me that over the phone?" Skepticism gripped him from all angles. He needed to be more careful who he spoke to now. He had been too oblivious all the rest of his life and look where it had gotten him!

Molly looked down to her coffee cup and picked at the edge of the lid. She sighed, then looked back up to Parker and held his suspicious gaze steadily. "I know you don't trust me. You have no reason to. But before your book came out, I believed the love of my life to be dead."

"As he thought you were, too."

"But I wasn't!"

"Well, obviously..." Parker pushed his plate away from him to signify he was done.

A smile pulled at one corner of Molly's mouth. She leaned across the table, too. "And anyway," she said quietly. "If I was one of the bad guys, I wouldn't have met you at a public place. If I had wanted to harm you, Parker, I would have already done it. I wouldn't be sitting here having a nice conversation with you over... whatever that is." She pointed to his plate of leftovers.

Parker sat back and also studied his plate. "Biscuits and gravy," he said. "You've never had biscuits and gravy?"

"I have not."

"It was delicious. You should try it sometime." He lifted his eyes to study the woman who sat across from him. She had good points about meeting in a public place and all...

"I'll... think about it," she said, giving his plate a skeptical look as she took another sip of her coffee.

"All right," Parker said at last. "Answer some of my questions... and then I'll answer some of yours."

She nodded. "Okay... what do you want to know?" She put up her hands as if she had nothing to hide.

"What happened to you? I only know your story from Greysen's perspective. If you read my book, then you know what I know. What happened to you after you went to Edrick's office?" He narrowed his eyes and watched her closely; how her eyes jetted around the place as if somebody might be watching her.

He noticed her behavior right away because it was exactly how he'd often felt since he'd written Greysen's story.

"I don't... I don't remember much because I was knocked out. But I woke up in a small room of sorts, like a panic room kind of. It didn't have anything in it... and they... they did—" She moved her voice down to a whisper. "Parker, they did horrible things to me. I didn't have anything to do with—" She stopped suddenly, visibly upset.

Parker glanced around the place to make sure nobody was listening in on them as she began to tremble slightly. He reached his hand across the table and placed it over the top of hers. "It's okay. You don't have to tell me. I understand." *Do I?*

"The thing is," she continued, still in a whisper, "I found out after a while that the panic room they'd put me in... was in Edrick's mansion."

A silence overcame them. Parker knew exactly what she was implying. "Oh my God... you were in the mansion the same time Greysen was," he whispered.

She stared at him, her brown eyes flecked with gold and a look of desperation in them. "I didn't know until I read your novel."

"I'm so sorry, Molly," he whispered back.

She shook her head. "There's no way he could have known."

Parker agreed with a firm shake of his head. "No way. He left town because he thought you were dead. No way he would have left without knowing you were safe, or if there was any possibility that you were still alive." Parker pulled his phone out of his pocket and lit it up, checking the time. He was still good. There was no way Nori was awake yet. He set the phone on the table in front of him.

"I know. I know he wouldn't have. Honestly, after I heard that explosion outside, which I now know was his car, I thought he was dead. Edrick told me he killed him. I lost all hope." She drew a deep, shaky breath, tears shining in her eyes. She paused a moment to compose herself, then cleared her throat. "You say he left town... where? Where did he go? Where is he now? The moment your novel hit the shelves and began to gain popularity, I knew I had to find you. Because I knew that story wasn't fiction. It was *my* story. Mine and Greysen's story."

Parker shifted in his chair. "Molly. I wish I could tell you where Greysen was." He saw her broken heart across the table in the quiver of her eyelid and the twitch in the corner of her lip. He didn't know how she'd escaped. But she was here, now, talking to him.

"But where did he go?" She was persistent, with a quirk in her voice that sounded almost irritated.

Parker hesitated, studying her again. Her heartbreak looked genuine. And anyway, he supposed he didn't really have all that much information to share. Even with the good guys.

"Well, I met him in Paris. He fled to France after everything that happened. He's been living as a homeless man."

She exhaled sharply. "Why? Why would he do that? He's living on the streets?"

Parker nodded. "He did it as a cover-up. There are so many homeless in Paris, it was a strong cover. Nobody would have looked twice at him."

She nodded. "He's the most intelligent man I've ever met."

Once again he saw the sadness in her eyes. "He is a good man, Molly." Parker pulled his hand away from hers and looked up at the old school clock that hung over the window at the coffee bar. "But did you really fly all the way from New York to ask me about Greysen's location?" This was partly a rhetorical question. *There's no way. She wants something else.*

She was quiet a moment, taking another sip of her coffee as if they were just meeting for a normal, everyday breakfast date. He thought he saw the fingers around the cup twitch. She held her composure, but Parker began to sweat. Perhaps what he'd seen as heartbreak before was actually nerves. She was clearly nervous.

He locked eyes with her.

"I'm being watched," she whispered. "And you probably are, too."

A shudder resonated throughout his entire body at the sound of her words. He wasn't expecting them. Of all the things she could have said, and all his paranoia of being followed lately, even still, hearing her formulate the words sent a chill through his bones. He sat back in his chair and only barely resisted the urge to look around the restaurant wildly. "What, like right now, as we sit here?" His voice pitched higher than normal, as if he had a croak in his throat. He didn't take his eyes off her, in fear that what he asked was true. He didn't want it to seem like they knew someone was there.

"I don't know about this very second," Molly said quietly. "In fact, I hope not, which is why I wanted to come to you in person. It seems to take them longer to catch up to me that way. I know, though, that I am being tracked. Edrick and his men know about Greysen and I, even though Greysen kept our lives together very private for fear of conflict-of-interest with our careers. They think he will find his way back to me, eventually."

"Which is what you want?"

Molly sighed, gazing down at her coffee thoughtfully. "I want to know he is safe. And of course, yeah, I'd love to be with him. But if me being with him means he's dead, then I want to know where he is, so I can stay far away. "

Parker hadn't considered that. "I recall you saying you thought Greysen was dead? Why would they follow you if you've thought this the whole time?"

"Well, Edrick knows he didn't kill Greysen. He knows he got away somehow. He doesn't know how, but he knows he's out there. And they think it's only a matter of time before he'd try to contact me. So they're watching my every move. I didn't know the truth about him myself until I saw your book. Saw you interviewed on TV."

"Are you sad he hasn't contacted you?" Parker asked.

Molly went quiet. "He can't contact a dead woman, right?"

She had a point. Just as much as she'd thought he was dead, Greysen thought the same about her.

"But I *am* frustrated he hasn't even tried."

"He went off the map." Parker shrugged. "You can't blame him. When you disappear, you know how it works. It's final."

She nodded. "Yeah I know."

Parker stole a moment to look around the cafe bar as another couple entered and ordered at the coffee shop counter. He saw no one suspicious, and eventually turned back to Molly. "Okay, but... what do they want with *me*? I see why they are keeping tabs on you. But why me? I'm just a kid from KC. I'm a nobody."

"You wrote *The Idea Man*."

He pursed his lips shut.

She continued, "You wrote the story of a man who is largely wanted by some very bad people. It's reasonable for them to assume you had contact with him to gather that information. And... and they think perhaps there's some sort of secret message in the text telling them to fuck off."

Parker narrowed his eyes. "How do you know so much about what they think?"

She didn't break his gaze. "I have somebody on the inside," she said, just above a whisper.

Parker scoffed and shook his head, then scraped his hands through his hair. "What in the..." He groaned. "How have I gotten myself into this mess?"

"Listen, Parker." Molly leaned forward. "You want my advice? You need to get out of here. You need to run. Go somewhere. Far away. If you want to stay out of this—then you need to run. Pretty soon they're going to figure out I came here and spoke to you. And it's not going to be good for either of us."

Parker's heart began to race. "Why did you come here then?" he demanded. "You brought the danger to me!"

Molly pursed her lips. Her eyebrows lifted. "You entered danger the moment you spoke to Greysen Price. Whether I came here or not, they will find you." She screeched her bar stool back and stood up, grabbing her purse off the chair. "It was a pleasure meeting you."

Parker's mouth dropped open. He couldn't believe she was just going to leave him like this. "Wait, so... we can work together as a team then, right? Protect each other?" It almost seemed like she'd just come here to try and get Greysen's location from him, or to see how much more he knew and that was that.

She stood a moment. "Just... please listen to me, Parker. And don't try to contact me again." With that, she turned on her heels and clicked her way out of the Opera House.

He stared after her for a long moment, waves of shock and confusion numbing him.

Well, what the hell do I do now? Parker put his head in his hands a moment, feeling the repercussions of his trouble sleeping through the sinus pressure under his eyes. *If only there was a way Greysen knew Molly was still alive. Maybe that could change everything! Greysen could bring Molly into hiding with him. Then, they're both protected, and they get to be together.* Molly had seemed into him still after all these years. He rose from the table at last and threw away his half-eaten tray. *But how can I find Greysen again?* He made it pretty clear the last time they met that they'd never see each other again.

He walked to the coffee counter and ordered a coffee and a scone for Noriana. Then, he watched the barista put the coffee together as if the world wasn't closing in on him.

But it was. It was narrowing and choking him, thoughts of where he could possibly go, what he was running from, why he was in this position in the first place—stirring up a storm of anxiety.

He thanked the barista and grabbed the coffee from the pick-up counter at the end. Then he pushed out the door into the frigid air. He wondered if Noriana was awake or not yet.

If she wasn't, he'd slip back into the apartment as softly as he'd left, and breakfast would be waiting for her when she woke. For now, he'd let her sleep. Because he had a feeling neither one of them was going to be getting much sleep from here on out.

FIVE

Parker placed both hands on Noriana's face, stared directly into her striking eyes, and said, "You know, we really don't have to do this. We can turn around right now. Get out of here. Run."

She pushed back from his chest and squinted at him, turning towards the house. "Cooome on. Meeting your parents can't be *that* bad." She marched up the driveway.

"They're not the ones I'm worried about," he mumbled as he rushed to catch up. Noriana wore a denim dress and yellow sweater today, with tan leather boots. He'd never seen her in a dress before. The skin from just below her knee to mid-thigh was exposed. His heart flipped in his chest. He swallowed, tried to focus. "My two brothers, Stephen and Marshall, are in there. I'm most nervous about them."

She chuckled. "Why?"

45

"We grew up together! They *know* things about me. And also I never bring girls home. In fact, I've never brought a girl home. Like ever." He shrugged.

"Are you serious?" she asked, almost a pang of nerves in her voice. She stopped on the porch and placed her hand on his chest.

"Don't worry about it." He placed his hand on top of hers. "I just haven't felt like I've ever liked a girl enough to introduce her to my family." He shrugged, again. "They never seem to last very long."

She cocked her head to one side, one eyebrow lifting up to hide behind her bangs. "And why's that?" She removed her hand and turned to the door.

"No, don't take offense to that!" He wedged himself between her and the door. "Honestly, Nori, it's just never worked out in the end." He took her hand in his and smiled down at her. "But I'm glad you get to meet them because now they'll believe I actually have a girlfriend, since we've been long distance and all."

She laughed. "They don't think I'm real? That's kind of sad..." She placed her hand on the small of his back.

He looked over his shoulder at her. "Oh, just wait." Without knocking, he pushed the front door open and let Noriana in before him.

As he'd expected, at the sound of the door opening, his mother promptly appeared. "Hi sweetie!" She entered the foyer and approached them, then crushed Parker into a hug. For such a petite woman, she had unexpected arm strength. Her slick blonde hair fell to her shoulders, and she tucked it behind one ear as she turned from him to face Noriana.

"Hey, Mom," Parker said when he could breathe again. "This is Nori."

A huge smile warmed his mom's face. "Hi Nori, it's so nice to finally meet you. You can call me Dottie. Welcome!" She folded Noriana into a hug as well, then motioned them inward. "Please come in. Come in!"

Parker looked over to Nori and raised his eyebrows, smiling as they meandered from the foyer into the living room.

"She *does* exist!" Marshall came into the room, heading straight for Noriana and picking her up, spinning her around.

"Marshall, seriously! Put my girlfriend down. Geeze."

He set her down and took a step back. "Bon jor! How-do-you-like-America so far?" He spoke slowly and clearly, with a terrible French accent, if it was even acceptable to call it that.

"She's *from* America, you idiot!" Parker interjected under his breath before slamming a punch into his brother's bicep.

"Marshall!" Dottie scolded as though he were twelve and not a grown man.

"I just want her to feel warmly welcomed!" he yelled out, rubbing the side of his arm.

"Oh, I feel so warm," she said jokingly, laughing alongside them.

Parker sighed. *At least she's a good sport.* He guided her to the dining room, where his mother already had dinner set out. His dad sat at the head of the table, and Stephen and his wife were there, too.

"Hey, Dad." Parker gave his Dad a one-armed hug. "This is Nori."

His Dad pushed back his seat and stood, leaning forward with his hand extended. He shook Noriana's hand with his other hand cupped over their shake. "Pleasure to meet you. Call me Davis."

Nori smiled at him as he sat back down, and she turned to the other two. "You must be the other brother?" she asked.

"Yeah, I'm Stephen and this is my wife Melissa." He stood and stretch over the table to shake her hand, Melissa following suit. Melissa was always there, at all of their family functions, but she was so quiet you'd hardly notice her. "Thought I'd keep it short since you'd already endured Marshall." He winked at Parker.

Parker smirked at his brother, relieved. Stephen was always the more mature one of the three. He pulled out Nori's chair for her and then sat down next to her.

Dinner was spaghetti and meatballs, with Italian bread and a garden salad, all made by his mom.

Parker was suddenly hit with a heavy sensation. An overwhelming feeling of how lucky and privileged he was to have this life. He had a family who loved him. Parents who lived in a beautiful home that would scoop in and rescue him at any given moment. Emotion crept up on him as he reached from the colander of pasta. It wasn't that he didn't deserve what he had, it was that *everyone* deserved to have this. *Greysen is just out there on the streets. Thinks everyone he loves is dead.* The overwhelming emotion transformed into guilt. Parker held the information Greysen needed to turn his life around.

"So Nori, how was your trip over? Have you ever been to Kansas City before?" Dottie asked

49

as they clanked dishes and served themselves, passing the food around in a circle.

Parker squeezed some ranch dressing onto his garden salad and looked over at Noriana. She seemed comfortable as she spread butter onto her bread, which put him at ease. He needed to tell her everything that had been going on, with Molly and what's been on his mind. Though watching her calm disposition, he knew she'd been understanding and supportive. He had no reason to doubt that. She'd understand that he needed to tell her on his own time.

"No, I've never been here before," she answered, setting down the butter knife in the butter tub and passing it to Parker's Dad to her left. "I'm living in Paris right now, but I'm from San Francisco." She twirled the spaghetti onto her fork and took a bite. "This is delicious!"

She seemed like a natural at this 'being social' thing.

Parker took the pitcher of ice water from his mom as she lit up. He poured his glass and set it on the table close to Noriana.

"Well thank you! I tried sautéing the onions first before putting them into the sauce this time."

"It's good, Dot." Parker's dad nodded from the other side of the table.

Parker hadn't been sure how Nori would react to meeting his family for the first time. Even though she wasn't a shy person by any means and could handle crowds, she didn't often like talking about herself. She'd told him once that she had social anxiety, but he'd never guess it from watching her. Perhaps because she'd had so much practice speaking to strangers while tour-guiding at the museums, something she had to learn to do while at the University. Though that was much different than small-talk conversation, of course, because while giving tours, she could talk about something she had a true passion for. And perhaps everyone had a little bit of social anxiety.

"How did you guys meet each other?" Parker's dad spoke up from the end of the table, his eyes squinting with glee behind his glasses.

Noriana spoke up before he got the chance to.

"Parker was stalking one of my tour groups at the Museum of Modern Art in Paris," Nori answered, glancing over at him with a mischievous smile.

He rolled his eyes ironically. "I was mesmerized by her voice."

Laughs erupted around the table.

51

"No seriously though, I went to the museum to—" It almost slipped that he'd been sent there from a stalker message that was left on his windshield by Greysen. His family knew nothing about what he'd been through, or the danger he was presently in. Perhaps even he didn't know the extent of it.

"—to people watch," Noriana finished. No doubt she'd noticed his hesitation.

"Aww, you guys even finish each other's sentences!" Marshall teased.

"Shut up, Marshall!" Parker fell into his trap. From childhood, it was known that if Parker ignored Marshall, he'd move on. React, and he'd be motivated to tease further. "I went to people watch for the novel I was writing, and I heard a tour group go by. Nori could tell I was American right away, I mean, who couldn't?"

They all laughed again.

"How sweet!" his mother boasted. "Nori, tell us about your schooling over there. How different is University in a foreign country as opposed to here?" she asked.

The conversation continued through dinner, and Parker did his best to contribute and participate as if everything were completely normal. As if he hadn't of had a very alarming conversation with Molly just that morning. As if there weren't possibly some very scary people out there looking for him. Or the fact that he'd thoroughly convinced himself throughout the course of their meal that it was his responsibility to deliver the news of Molly back to Greysen, regardless the risk it may put him in. He was already in too deep.

When they had all finished their meal, Parker pushed his chair back, just as the rest of his family rose to help pick up dishes and bring them to the kitchen.

"I'll be right back, gonna go to the bathroom," he told Noriana as he turned and went down the hall. Just as he was about to reach the bathroom, a voice called out behind him.

"Hey bro!" It was Stephen, who hadn't said much over dinner.

Parker turned and offered his brother an apologetic smile. "Stephen, I have to piss really badly, good to see you though, man, it's been a while."

Stephen nodded. "Yeah it has, huh? Listen. This will be fast, I don't want Marshall or Mom overhearing me." He glanced over his shoulder to be sure the aforementioned people were not within earshot.

Parker tensed. "Okay?" Had his brother noticed his demeanor at dinner was off?

Stephen turned back to him, his hazel eyes serious, but compassionate. "Look. If you need help with anything, you let me know, okay?"

Parker clenched his jaw and then relaxed. Stephen was an emergency room doctor. He'd always been the star of the family. Parker felt he could never live up to Stephen, especially since he'd decided to pursue an English degree with a writing emphasis. And the fact that he'd had no job after college except to write. It was a big triumph for him to finish a novel and have it published and be a big hit, but it still didn't compare to Stephen's PhD in medicine and his perfect wife and his perfect job as an ER doctor at the University of Kansas Hospital.

"What are you talking about, bro?" Parker asked, trying to pry out what he knew.

Stephen reached up and pinched the bridge of his nose, then looked up. "Listen, Parker. You aren't acting like yourself. I know it's not because you're just bringing a girl here for the first time. I've known you my whole life, and I can tell something just isn't right. If you're in trouble, you don't have to tell me. Just know that I'm here for you if you need anything, okay? You can call if you need me."

Parker leaned against the wall, observing the photos of him and his brothers playing in one of those blue plastic pools in the backyard when they were little. His mom kept lots of such photos in a framed collage on the hallway wall.

"Thanks, man," Parker said, looking to the floor. He wished he could tell him. It would be nice to have another person aware of what had happened to him, and what could possibly happen. It could be a benefit to have another ally. But Stephen was so busy with his own life. Now was not the time or place... "I seriously appreciate that." He looked back into Stephen's face, who had that concerned doctor expression in his eyes. "There is... something." It slipped before he had the chance to wrangle it back.

Stephen leaned into him, "oh?"

"Nori is headed back to Paris tomorrow... and I'm—I'm going with her."

"That's grea—"

Parker held out his hand to stop him, closing his eyes a moment and then opening them again. "Nobody knows yet. Not even Nori. I have some unfinished business there. It...could be dangerous."

Stephen furrowed his brow but kept his mouth shut.

"I can't say much right now. But man," he held his hand up to his chest. "I'm just relieved to have told someone. My mind is going a little crazy."

Stephen clasped his hand on Parker's shoulder. "I got your back. You call if there's anything I can do. Even if you need an ear, okay?"

Parker nodded, his eyes welling with tears. He turned his head and sniffed, rubbing under his nose.

"Alright, go piss," Stephen said, hesitated a moment in the hallway, then turned and headed back towards the kitchen.

Parker did his business, composed himself, and then rushed back to the kitchen, aware of the time he'd been away from Noriana. He didn't want to leave her alone with his family for *too* long, this being the first time they'd met and all. He turned the corner, where she and his mom were loading dishes into the dishwasher.

"I like her, Parker, she helps out in the kitchen!" his mom teased.

He walked up to Noriana and placed his hands around her hips.

"Yeah, you don't help your mom out in the kitchen?" Noriana teased as well, leaning her head back against his chest to look up at him accusingly.

56

"I do, too!" he insisted, feigning offense. "Marshall doesn't."

"Hey watch it, buddy, you don't want to start that war!" Marshall yelled out from the living room.

"We should probably go, though. Mom, thanks for dinner. It was delicious."

"Aww, you can't stay longer?" she asked, wiping her hands on a towel.

"I'm afraid not. Noriana doesn't have much time left in Kansas City and we have some things to take care of." He let go of Nori, stepping away from her to grab the parmesan cheese from the counter and put it into the fridge. He'd hoped the excuse sounded totally normal. Tonight, he'd have the chance to catch Nori up.

Sounds of the Chiefs game resounded into the kitchen. His father and brothers were in the TV room watching the football game. The familiar vibrations of the house, and the calm of his family working together and spending time together, reminded him of the daunting possibilities of what lay ahead. He couldn't help but think this was probably the calmest he would feel for a long time to come.

His mother sighed. "Well, all right then." She moved across the kitchen to give him a peck on the cheek and that wistful look she always got before he left her house again. "Don't be a stranger!"

Parker said his goodbyes to the rest of his family and hurried Noriana out before the guilt could get any worse. After all, he hadn't told any of them besides Stephen, that he would be back on an airplane to France in the morning.

SIX

Noriana sat on the edge of her twin bed in the tiny dorm room on the University de Sorbonne campus in Montmartre, her head in her hands.

"Ah c'mon, don't be upset," Parker reassured her, sitting on the edge of the bed next to her. "We talked about this. The entire time on the seven-hour plane ride. I thought you were on board." He rubbed her thigh.

The small dorm room was no bigger than the bathroom of his parent's house back home, with only room for two beds across from each other, and dresser drawers at the end of each one. A desk leaned up against the wall between the beds. He could only assume shared bathrooms and a community room that held a kitchen and a sitting area were down the hall.

"I'm just scared for you, Parker," Noriana whispered. "And you hardly know *any* French!" She looked up at him with red eyes.

"Are you really this upset about me going out there on the streets?" he asked.

She nodded. "I know it's probably the only way to find Greysen, though. But isn't there some way I can be here for backup if you need help?"

Parker shook his head. "He needs to know his girl is alive. The whole reason he left and assumed a new identity was because he thought she was dead! I can't let him go on thinking that. I just can't. What if there's a chance him and Molly could be together?" He took her hands from her lap and squeezed them. "And you will help me the most by staying right here. I don't want to expose you to more danger," he said quietly.

She scoffed a laugh. "I have been exposed to this since day one!"

He paused a moment, then added, "Plus, for this to really work, I need the full immersion of being on the streets. I can handle myself, really."

"Really?" she asked, the inflection in her voice revealing she wasn't so convinced.

"I've been practicing my French." He smirked.

"Let's hear it, then." She smiled, freeing her hands from his, then leaned over on her bed and pushed open her one window, allowing some of the cool air to waft into the room.

"Uh, est-que tu connaitre ou l'homme appele Greysen?"

Despite her efforts, Noriana couldn't keep a straight face.

"What?" he demanded.

"It's okay, babe. It's okay." She patted his shoulder. She hesitated a moment, her long lashes pointed to the floor. She heaved a sigh and then spoke, "You better get out of here before Charlotte gets back."

He stood from the bed, gently pushing her hair off her shoulder.

He'd never met Noriana's roommate, Charlotte, before, but he also couldn't imagine fitting even one more person in that room. He also didn't know what the rules were about having non-students stay with you in your room.

"I'll catch up to you, okay?" he told her, studying her face. Her high cheek bones, her red lips, her straight bangs. "This is not goodbye."

She reached her hand up to his cheek and leaned into him.

He pushed into her, kissing her harder than he had since that night in the Bed and Breakfast in Versailles last year. He kissed her as if it would be the last time he'd get the chance to.

SEVEN

The truth was, he'd played it cool back there in Noriana's dorm room, but he was terrified. How was he, Parker Rubec, supposed to make it in the streets and back alleys of a foreign country? He didn't know the half of what it was like to suffer, or even feel uncomfortable with his basic needs: food, water, shelter, sleep.

Before he went out on his immersion search for Greysen, he sat outside a small café with a coffee that he'd used the last few coins in his pocket to get. A pen and paper sat on the table in front of him. This was a necessary pit stop before he moved forward. He began to write:

"Dear Noriana,

If you are reading this letter, it probably means that I am gone. I am about to embark on a task that may get me killed. This may be the last thing I ever get to say to you..."

It crossed his mind that perhaps he was being a little dramatic. Did he really think he could die posing as a homeless person to find Greyson? No... this letter wasn't for that. This letter and the letter he was about to write to his Mom afterward, were for the end of this whole thing, if he didn't make it—which at this rate was a possibility. His fingers clutched the pen as he wrote the words. His goodbyes.

A knot caught in his throat as he imagined the task at hand. This experience would be artificial. He was only pretending to be homeless, as opposed to the countless people living on the streets with no other option. Living his privileged life, he could never understand what it felt like to be on the bottom. Oftentimes people from the upper and middle class looked down upon the poor as if it was their fault they were in that position.

Even though he was posing as a homeless person to try and find Greysen, and he would experience what it was like to sleep on the street, he would never understand what it really felt like to be stuck there. While he'd be experiencing hunger and cold and discomfort, in the back of his mind he'd always know that if at any moment he couldn't take it anymore, he could go home. Other people didn't have that choice.

He finished the letters, then meticulously folded them and placed them in his pocket. It was only mid-day, and his stomach already felt like it was eating away at itself from the inside.

He left the café and walked down the road. The smells of fresh bread and open-walled Brasserie's wafted under his nose, making his belly ache even more. He walked with his hands in his pockets, his hoodie zippered up to his neck. His nose was already numb, and if anything, the biggest challenge would be the natural elements.

It was bitter cold in winter. He was lucky so far that it hadn't actually snowed, but it didn't need to for him to feel the aggressive bite in the wind. He was bound to get sick.

His nose was already starting to run.

He rubbed his stomach and walked along the cobblestoned sidewalk, peeking down every street and alley as he went.

During the day, it was hard to determine the homeless from other people walking around the city. So many people walked the streets of Paris, and everyone seemed to have a destination. If you didn't act like you knew where you were going, you could be a target.

Parker walked all the way from Montmartre to the North train station Gare du Nord, the place where his story had begun in Paris. He didn't know his odds of finding Greysen here, but it was worth a shot. It had been the place he'd first met the man.

It was ideal for people watching. That's what had attracted him to it before. Only this time, with his mission at hand, he headed straight for the bathrooms in the underground. Not for the toilets, but for the panhandlers.

He'd seen them last time and brushed them away when they'd asked him if he wanted to purchase any metro tickets from them. Why would he buy metro tickets off those men when he could just go a few feet into the underground and buy them from the vending machine, or the ticket vendor in the window?

They were probably cheaper. But they were also probably counterfeit. They most likely just needed some money for a meal. Or to provide for a family.

Parker sighed and shook his head. He needed to stop assuming things. To stop stereotyping people. He didn't know how it was, or what they might be suffering. He would never know what it felt like to really be in their shoes.

He treaded down the ceramic-tiled stairs into the underground. The cement gray walls felt as though they were closing in on him, and he lifted his hand up to brush his throat.

Breathe, Parker... breathe. His nerves were getting to him. And he wasn't sure if it was from the stress of not being able to speak the language, or if he was afraid of approaching these people on their turf and what they might do to him. Or the possibility that none of this would lead him to Greysen.

He spotted the two men before they saw him.

One was younger than him, probably around nineteen-years-old or so, the other was older, though they didn't look like they had any relation to each other. They were both wearing old, tattered clothes, and the older of the two men wore an oversized, brown winter jacket.

"Excusez-moi—," Parker spoke from behind them in a low, non-confident tone.

They didn't hear him and continued plotting out something in another language other than French. It sounded Arabic. There were quite a few people in France from Egypt. Noriana had told him a quarter of the population of students in her classes were from Egypt.

"Salut," Parker tried again, "uhh, I uhh, Je parle francais un petite peu." He didn't know what to say to these men, so he muttered the only sentence he knew well that he had on auto pilot: *Hi, I speak French a little bit.*

The older man strung out a series of words in French that were too fast for him to understand. The younger man stepped in, holding up the fake metro tickets and speaking quickly again.

Parker backed up and shook his hands in front of him as if to decline.

The men yelled more foreign words at him and shooed him away, turning away from him.

"No!" Parker insisted, "I need to talk to you!"

"No Enlash," the younger man spat.

"What then? No Arabic either." Parker immediately regretted saying such a thing as soon as he said it. He was once again stereotyping. What if they weren't Egyptian at all? He was a dead man. The language barrier was his downfall. *What am I doing?*

In the most broken French he could muster, he asked the men if he could talk to them for a moment about if they'd seen somebody.

"Vous policier?" the older of the two men asked.

Parker mumbled under his breath, "Pol...icier. Police?" If it wasn't obvious what this word sounded close to, he also remembered it from the accidental time he'd spent behind bars during their trip to Versailles. "Hell no!" he laughed, trying to think of the next thing to say.

Right about now would be a great time to have his phone. The thing could translate a word on a sign just when you hovered over it with the camera. Or convert conversations in real time. But for this process to even artificially work, he'd had to leave his phone back at Noriana's dorm. He wouldn't allow himself a device that could get him out of here the moment things got tough. The temptation to use it and rely on the phone the way he did in his everyday life was just too high. He needed to do this thing on his own.

The next string of communication from the guy was a mixture of sounds and inflection. Context told Parker the older gentleman thought if he wasn't a customer, and he wasn't the police, that perhaps he was trying to take their territory. He wasn't happy about it. Parker gathered that the underground was most likely very organized in the panhandling circuit. He didn't really want to know any more about it than that.

He found the younger man's French was just as bad as his own. So, both of them spoke a sort of mixed French. Parker's was what Noriana liked to call "Franglais", which was slang for French

69

with English words mixed in wherever he couldn't think of the French word fast enough.

"Avez vous un homme. Il s'appelle Grey—" He stopped in his tracks. If Greysen was smart, and he very much was, he wouldn't go by his real name. Parker had never asked him what name was on his fabricated passport. He used his hands to demonstrate to scratch that sentence and started over. Parker got straight to the point and asked if they'd seen a man matching Greysen's description.

They shook their heads no.

Parker put his head down and was about to take off when the younger of the two gentlemen grabbed his shoulder. He looked up, his eyes landing on a map enclosed in a case on the wall. He followed the man's motions over to it. He watched as the man pointed to several locations on the map; high tourist areas, and bridges cascading over the Seine River.

"Merci. Thanks!" He nodded to the men, then turned and ran for the stairs.

The sun was setting on the horizon of the city, allowing the sky to bleed an orangish glow behind the backdrop of the historic buildings. He could try to go to Notre Dame first, remembering back to the first time he'd met Greysen. Greysen had claimed a lamppost right outside the beautiful, historic cathedral.

But it was getting darker, and soon it would be hard to see anything. He needed to find a place to sleep. He followed the street to the first bridge that crossed the Seine River in all of its glory.

The Seine was a landmark of Paris that often got overshadowed by the huge museums or the Eiffel Tour, which brought in thousands of tourists each year.

Parker couldn't understand why everyone would want to go to a giant metal landmark when the natural beauty of the river was right there. The current lapped over itself like molten lava, and he imagined it must have been colder than the air that left his skin feeling raw.

He reached up and rubbed his eyes, then walked along a cement wall that led to a staircase down to the bank of the river.

His knees felt weak as he went down the stairs. Every muscle in his body felt as though it would collapse, simply from one day of exposure to the elements.

It's just one night, Parker... just one night. Get over this hump and you'll be alright. These people don't get a choice. You at least have a choice.

His sore body moved down the stairs to the landing next to the River. Now he just needed to find a bridge he felt safe sleeping under, that wasn't already claimed territory. He was sure that some of the homeless went to a shelter of some sort for night time, but Greysen wouldn't do that. Greysen would feel like he didn't deserve a shelter. He was continuing to punish himself for something he didn't really have that much control over.

As Parker continued to walk towards the first underpass, he thought he saw the shadows of a few bodies tucked under the bridge.

When he'd previously taken a boat ride during vacation, he had seen that some of the underpasses of the bridges had old, dirty mattresses, or stacked newspapers to make a floor under them. He wasn't sure if his eyes were failing him or not; if he was just seeing the shapes of people because that's what his eyes were wanting to see, or if they were really there.

As he got closer, he confirmed that there were indeed people on the mattress under that bridge. They didn't notice him as he got closer, and as he neared them, he started to go over in his mind what he should say to them. Perhaps if there wasn't any room for him to stay the night here, he should still ask them if they'd seen

Greysen. That was the whole point of him being out here, right?

When he neared them, he saw it was a man and a woman and as she turned towards him, he caught a glimpse of something.

What in the...?

He saw her bare breast as the man pushed into her from behind, grabbing her on the shoulder and rocking back and forth.

"Shit!" Parker yelled, startling the two of them.

He hadn't been expecting to walk in on people having sex in these circumstances. The woman hissed at him, something in French, and when she opened her mouth Parker cringed at the small, dirty nubs that hung inside her lips.

He put his hands up in defense and walked sideways passed the mattress. He put his head down and continued to walk, hearing them laugh like hyenas behind him. He preferred the laughing to the groaning that had been going on just moments ago.

He continued to walk until his legs were numb. It was cold. He was hungry. He was tired. He came upon another underpass that seemed to be deserted. There was nothing but a ripped, grimy, thin blanket that looked like it had been taken from an airplane. How ironic for him.

He crawled up onto the ledge that was just feet from the cold, green metal of the bridge. He left the blanket on the surface underneath, in case its owner would be back for it, and curled up into a ball, hugging his knees close to his chest. His face was raw, his breath visible in the air, and his hands shook.

What am I doing... this was a mistake.

His gut swirled with anxiety. His aching stomach wasn't cramping anymore, as it was beyond hunger and seemingly in hibernation mode now. But next came the nausea.

Emotion balled up in his throat, and he didn't have the energy to keep it in place. He began to cry into his chest with blubbery shudders, the best he could with what little energy he had left to muster.

"Premiere fois?"

A small, quiet voice spoke out behind him. He hadn't heard anybody approach, but that could have been because of the sobbing noises he was making into the side of the bridge. As mucus poured out of his nose, it seemed to just freeze the moment it touched the air, crusting on his upper lip.

He didn't want to turn around to see who was there. He didn't have the energy to try and deal with transforming his words into something that this other person could understand, English or not. He heard a loud sigh, and then the touch of something heavy was placed on his side. He flinched, looking over to see the person had blanketed him with their coat. It wasn't the nicest smelling jacket, with the scent of musty exhaust, but it instantly warmed him on his shoulders and ribs.

Who was this decent soul who'd come out of nowhere? Why were they being so nice to him? Why did they offer their coat off their own back on such a cold night? Was he *that* pathetic looking?

He turned to catch a glimpse of the savior, to let them know the best he could that he was grateful for them. The silhouette of a man stood there, outlined by moonlight dancing off the river. A familiar silhouette.

I'm hallucinating. This can't be real. This isn't real. Parker pushed himself up sitting and opened his mouth to try and form words but his throat cracked.

The man came closer and squinted as he peered into Parker's face, then his own face went slack, losing all its color.

"Parker! What the hell, man!?" Greysen leaped up onto the ledge and threw his arm around Parker. "What are you doing here? How'd you get here? You look freezing cold!"

Parker couldn't believe this was happening. He couldn't believe after all of this, his plan had worked. He'd found the man he sought to find. Out of all the odds, here he sat.

Regardless of if this was a hallucination or not, Parker had never been happier to see that scruffy faced, gray-haired, beast of a man. "I... I was looking for you. I wasn't sure if you were still here in Paris or not."

"So you go and curl yourself up under a bridge? I don't understand how you got from A to B!" Greysen stifled a laugh and shook his head.

They sat there a moment, shoulder to shoulder, feet dangling over the ledge. Parker shook as he saw his breath in the air. He was asking himself that same question.

How did *I get from A to B...?*

His world twinkled. Parker grabbed the edges of the musty jacket and pulled it over his neck. The warmth of the garment was just enough to bring back a tingling feeling in his fingers, but his vision continued to spin.

Is Greysen even real?

There wasn't much left to contemplate as black seeped in around the edges of his vision.

The world was slipping away from him. Further and further away.

But he felt comforted now. Safe in the arms of someone who seemed to be able to navigate situations like this far better than he could.

Perhaps it would be better if he gave in and allowed the world to swallow him whole...

Then blackness.

EIGHT

He blinked his eyes open, and his vision fell upon the light blue textured ceiling. His entire body ached, and he turned to his side, moaning as he moved.

"Good morning."

The voice startled him, and he turned with all his might to see who leaned against the wall towards the end of his bed.

"Greysen, I thought I dreamed you up last night. Geeze. Am I still in a dream?" His voice was hoarse and he mustered a small cough to clear his throat.

"No, you're not dreaming. You're lucky I found you," Greysen said quietly. "There's a cup of peppermint tea on the side of your bed."

Greysen didn't have to tell him twice. Parker reached out and grabbed the cup. He sipped the top the best he could, and closed his eyes as the soothing, warm liquid shimmied down his throat. He took a quick glance around the small, barren yet cozy room. *Where are we? Greysen must have contacts everywhere.* "Thank... thank you. Again. For everything." He looked up at Greysen. He had so many questions. But the most pressing one wanted to explode out of him. "I needed to find you. I thought the only way would be to try and walk in your shoes. I hardly even lasted one night. How do people do this all the time?"

"They have no choice."

Parker pursed his lips. He allowed the words to sink in deep.

"What brought you back to Paris, anyway?" Greysen asked, crossing his arms over his gray, long-john shirt that most likely wasn't gray when it was new. "How is Nori doing? You kids still together?"

Parker felt anxious with the small talk because he wanted to get straight to the point, but it was also comforting that he could have a conversation with Greysen again. He thought he'd never see the man ever again. "Yeah, we're still going together. She's great. She told me she hadn't seen you since I left Paris, which made me scared that you had moved on."

"Hm." Greysen bit his lip.

Parker watched him contemplate what he'd just said. *I'm so lucky. I probably just caught him before he was going to take off!* He took another sip of the peppermint tea. The next thought flooded into his mind as a throb at his temples. "Greysen... there's something I need to tell you." His throat caught again. The information was burning to come out. "I don't know how else to put this... I guess I'll just come right out and say it." He took a deep breath, exhaled, and said it. "Molly, she's alive."

He saw the man absorb his words, sinking back into the wall of the small room.

"To hear ... to hear someone say those words," Greysen rasped. His eyes shone with tears. "I've waited so long to hear that, Parker. How can you be sure?"

"Well, I ate breakfast with her last week in Kansas City."

Greysen heaved a big sigh and rubbed his face. Then shook his head. "I wasn't... Well, I'd been living so many years thinking I'd been responsible for her death, as you know. Recently... there's been a development that led me to believe what you just told me could be true. But I thought it was a ploy to get me to turn myself in. I didn't know what to believe. I have so much to tell you, Parker."

"Hold on. Slow down." He sat up straight, both hands bracing himself on the bed. "Greysen... I was happy to help you get your story out there and everything. You know I didn't even want to take the advance you offered. It was very nice, though. I mean, it's improved my life by a million, but I can't get back into this. My meeting with Molly wasn't particularly... happy. She said I need to get away. To hide. That people are going to come after me because they think since I wrote your book, I have contact with you, so they want me to get to you." His words toppled one over the other. He didn't know where he was mustering the energy from, except that he needed to express how he felt.

Greysen shifted on his feet and stuck his hands into the pockets of his grimy pants. He gazed at Parker for a moment almost sadly, then shook his head. "I hate to tell you this, but I think you are beyond *wanting* to get out of this." He paused, and the heater in the small room rattled as it kicked on. "And for that, I am truly sorry. But I'm also so grateful for you."

Parker didn't know what to say to that. A multitude of emotions tumbled in his chest, everything from anger--at himself *and* Greysen for dragging him into this--to fear at the finality in Greysen's voice, to guilt for not feeling braver in this situation, for even having the desire to just run and let Greysen and Molly fend for themselves.

His clothes felt stiff as they hung on his body. He craved a shower. And food would have been nice. Once again that guilt hit him right in the gut. He'd spent literally one day on the streets and it'd been the roughest night of his life.

"I know you're sorry," he muttered finally under his breath. His hand dangled beside him on the bed and patted the side of his pocket. The quiet crinkle told him the letters he'd written, the only thing he currently possessed on his body aside from his clothes, were still there. Though a tad dramatic before, they seemed totally relevant now. He wasn't out of the woods. He wasn't in the clear of potentially having to have them delivered to Noriana and his mom.

"I think Molly," His voice cracked as though it'd be a long time since he'd formed her name on his tongue. "telling you to get away is right," Greysen said quietly after another moment of silence. "You need to go into hiding until all of this dies down, Parker. I wouldn't be able to forgive myself if something happened to you on my behalf—which seems to be a pattern with people I associate with. I thought maybe we'd changed the story just enough to make it unrecognizable. I mean, you marketed it as fiction. But the people involved knew exactly where it was coming from. And that's because they'd been looking for any sign of my existence." He paused abruptly, then asked, "You hungry?"

A quiet tap on the door followed his question.

How did he know someone was there? Parker watched Greysen walk to the door and open it just a crack, before grabbing a tray from someone and thanking them quietly.

He pulled the tray into the room and closed the door. He brought it to a small pull-out table at the end of the bed and lifted the silver lids. The delicious smell of breakfast filled the room.

"Where are we, anyway?" Parker asked, furrowing his brow. He should have asked sooner. He couldn't remember how he'd ended up here from last night after collapsing. "Do you have contacts everywhere?"

Greysen stifled a small chuckle. "I do. We are at a hotel on the outskirts of the Eighteenth Arrondissement. The owner is a friend of mine, and he will keep his word as to whether or not we've ever been here. He helped me out a lot when I first arrived in Paris. He was surprised to see me here last night because of my refusal of allowing him to offer me hospitality in the past."

Parker turned in the bed and stood up, walking his sore body over to the little table. He picked up a piece of jam toast and scoffed it down.

"Thank you." He nodded to Greysen. Something Greysen had said earlier was weighing on him. He'd said there had been some developments that led him to thinking Molly may have been alive. If she didn't know where he was, how could this be true? Perhaps he could help Greysen from falling into a trap. After everything Greysen had done for him, that's the last thing he wanted. He looked down at the plate of food. "After I get some more of this in my belly—" he swallowed a mouthful, "you wanna tell me about some of these developments you were talking about?" He reached for some bacon on the side of the plate.

Greysen nodded. "Yes. You need to know this. And it is time."

After eating his fill, Parker made a trip down the hall to the shared toilets. On his way back, he walked slowly, observing the patterned wallpaper and red carpet on the floor, and considering the war of dread and curiosity currently knotting up his insides. He heard a man and woman arguing in French downstairs. This place was dark with dimmed lights, and the hallways narrow with low ceilings. He wondered how many drug deals and prostitutes were brought through this place. But he was also grateful for its current sanctuary. The writer in him stirred up so many different stories of the histories in these walls.

And also so many possibilities for what Greysen was about to tell him.

He put the key in their door and slowly made his way back inside, apprehensive, but mostly ready to hear what Greysen had been meaning to share with him.

NINE

When Parker got back to the room, Greysen was still sitting at the small fold-out table by the bed, his head hung low.

"So you know how I said I had an inkling that Molly was alive this whole time but I didn't know for sure?" Greysen asked once Parker had shut and locked the door behind him.

Parker nodded.

"I have reason to believe she's been leaving signs for me. Physical signs."

Parker blinked at this news and took a seat on the edge of the bed. "Here? In Paris? How would she know you were here?"

Greysen scratched the stubbly, graying hairs on his chin. "Many years back, Molly and I had to take a business trip here. And it..." He looked down as though something had caught in his

87

throat. He grabbed a ceramic mug that sat on the table and took a sip before continuing.

Parker didn't dare say anything. The tension in the room could be cut with a knife. He was aware that Greysen was reliving some things as he told this story. And once again, just like he had when he wrote the first book, he listened.

Greysen continued, "That business trip was the first time we fell in love." He looked over at Parker and sighed. "There'd been a lot of attraction between us back home, but Molly is such a professional woman. She would have never acted on anything. Of course we worked closely with each other, but because of her professionalism and how she acted towards me at the office, I would have thought she hadn't even thought twice of me. That I was just a sorry divorcee that had screwed up his marriage. We were sent lots of different places for business trips, and we really got to know each other on the road. She was such a cool girl. There was no way she would go for somebody like me."

He stopped for a moment and sipped from the mug again. His blue gaze stared at the wall ahead, but the look in his eyes was far away.

"Well," he continued then, "one time we were sent on an assignment here, to Paris. And it just sort of happened. We had some time to kill after

88

one of our meetings one day and so we explored the Luxembourg Gardens. It's so beautiful. Just a wooded alcove, so private, so peaceful and away from the rest of the world. We'd had some sort of sexual tension all day long, knocking the back of our hands against each other accidentally as we walked, and... and," he laughed to himself, "...we'd got into a conversation about our past lovers. We stumbled upon this water fountain, called De Medici Fountain, have you seen it?"

Parker shook his head. "I should check it out. I'm from the city of fountains after all... Kansas City," he trailed off. It wasn't his time to speak now. It was his time to listen. "What happened at the fountain, Greysen?" he asked, with a half-smile on his lips.

"Well... she kissed me and my whole world changed."

There was another pause between them. Parker didn't know what to say.

Greysen gave a small shrug and continued, "The history behind the fountain is that it's a sculpture depicting the doomed lovers, Galatea and Acis. They are sharing one last embrace before Polyphemus, a very jealous god, tells them that will be the last time they are together."

Parker frowned. "That's sad. How is that romantic?"

"We always related it back to our situation. After that first day, where we found our love for each other at that fountain, whenever we had to come back here for business we would visit that fountain. You know our whole relationship had been kept secret? It was against company policy for us to have relations while we worked together at Humavision. I've always been a private person to begin with, keeping my personal life and work life separate, but our relationship needed to be kept secret for my protection, and especially for hers. We could relate with Galatea and Acis, because we felt like every time we had to sneak away, like we did that first day in the unmanicured and untamed trees and foliage of the alcove, it might be the last time we embraced and were together before we went back into the real world, where we couldn't express our true feelings."

"That's beautiful," Parker whispered, staring off into the ancient crown molding that lined the perimeter of the ceiling.

Greysen chuckled. "Anyway, since I came back here, I've visited De Medici Fountain many times when I'm missing her. A few weeks ago, I was there alone, and... and I noticed two roses laying on the edge of the fountain."

"Why two roses?" Parker asked.

"That was our thing!" Greysen explained. "Ever since we started seeing each other, I would always give her roses. Two. Two roses. Because one time she told me she was never interested in flowers, that it was a waste of money and she'd rather a guy do the dishes than buy her flowers that were going to die in a few days anyway. She'd rather the flowers live longer and stay in the ground. So as a joke, instead of a dozen roses, I got her two. To be funny. And she loved it. I mean... she didn't outright tell me she loved it, but I could tell." He smiled.

"You think she was here recently?" Parker asked, continuing to keep his voice low.

"I don't know. When I saw those roses, I knew she must be here, somehow. I didn't know if it was possible. And quite honestly, I thought I had hallucinated those roses at first. I'd wanted it so bad. But as you know, the reason I gave up looking for her and went on the run was because I was certain she was gone. Because of me. I couldn't handle that. And then to see those roses meant there was a possibility she was alive. And to think she was so close to me..." He shook his head and scrubbed his hands over his face.

"And then there was the part of me that thought maybe somebody else put them there. But nobody knows the story of us and the roses, so I don't know…"

Parker shifted on the edge of the bed and the mattress springs creaked a little. He cleared his throat. He didn't want to upset Greysen any more than he already was, but there had been something weighing on his mind ever since he'd met with Molly himself at Opera House. And Greysen needed to consider it, as difficult as it might be. He took a breath. "Greysen, you don't think…" He hesitated. How to put it delicately? "Now don't get mad…"

Greysen looked up at him, arching an eyebrow.

"Promise you won't get mad?"

Greysen frowned. "What do you mean? Why would I be mad? Come on now, just spit it out."

Parker did so, the words tumbling out so quickly he really did all but spit them out. "Do you think maybe she somehow could be working for Edrick now?" Then he rushed onward before Greysen could protest. "I got some suspicions when I met her for breakfast. It was a weird feeling, Greysen… I mean, yeah, you were in love and everything, but she was really pressing on where you were hiding. And my only defense for not blowing your cover was simply the fact that I truthfully had no idea where you were! And she got genuinely angry with me that I wouldn't give her that information."

Silence met his words. The corner of Greysen's lip twitched. He never seemed to act directly on emotion, something for which Parker was grateful for at that moment. "It's possible," Greysen whispered at last. "But I refuse to believe she's working for them on her own accord. It has to be against her will. She's forced to comply because they have some kind of hold on her."

Parker was relieved that he was a logical man and wasn't going to just act on his feelings. He'd been through too much to give himself up on a feeling.

Greysen broke the silence again. "But here's where it gets interesting..."

"Oh, it hasn't gotten to the interesting part yet!" Parker sat up straighter.

"I was walking by some shops and cafes down Boulevard Saint Germain, where your apartment had been, and when I was passing by this bar that had a few TVs outside on the front patio, I saw him."

"Him?"

"Edrick. On the TV."

A chill slinked by Parker's neck. The draft must have come from underneath the door, as there were no windows in the room. And he suddenly felt claustrophobic.

"He was on CNN doing some world technology innovation, convention thing. So I sat in. I watched the news story and he was talking about the recovery of his company and bringing it back up from the 'technology crash', he was calling it. I'm telling you, this man is a cockroach." He rose from his seat and began to pace the small area. "Even if you chop off his head he doesn't die. Anyway, he was talking about some blueprints he said he recovered from the collapse because they were in physical form and not digital. And my heart sank because I knew right then what he was talking about. I had some classified blueprints of a few inventions that I never wanted to see the light of day because of their potential for a lot of damage." He shook his head and looked to the ground. He rubbed his eyes a moment before continuing. "I should have never developed them to the point they were left at, but I had Edrick's iron fist hanging over my head, and if I didn't do it, he would have found someone else. However, I was able to divert him from those plans into other ones that better suited my

94

intentions." He sat on the edge of the bed and leaned forward, putting his elbows on his knees and his hands in his hair. "Especially after what I'd been through working for that man, I knew if he got a hold of any of my blueprints and actually built prototypes for them, I'd be screwed. We're all screwed. He'd just started to explain his future plans before one of the servers came out and shooed me away. Sometimes I forget I look like a raggedy, old homeless man. Shop owners don't want a stinky poor man hanging around their establishment, scaring away customers. But I had seen enough. All that I needed to know. And let me tell you, if he has his hands on the blueprints of the device I think he does, it's the worst thing that could happen." He looked up at Parker with fear and desperation.

Parker blinked, leaning forward toward Greysen on the bed. "Well? You gonna tell me what it is? The invention?"

Greysen looked to the floor, pursing his lips.

"Greysen!"

The man sighed. "You *are* the only one I have been able to talk to about this stuff," he mumbled. "Now, granted, these were just plans. It wasn't actually developed. So, you know how all of us humans have the same fate? In the end, we all die. The hope is that it is of old age after living a long, fulfilling, healthy life. So, say people are old and about to die, but they have so much knowledge on specific things; a lifetime full of knowledge and memories and experiences. You ever heard the expression 'I wish I knew then, what I know now'?" Greysen stood again, gesturing with his hands.

Parker sat on the edge of his seat against the wall, hanging on to Greysen's every word. He watched Greysen and it was almost like he saw the man glowing from his idea. As though he'd been suppressed for so many years. *He had been.*

Greysen continued, "Well, I worked off of that concept. And I developed a device that can record brain waves and then enable others to extract and translate these waves into knowledge. Ideas and memories."

Parker leaned back, trying to absorb this momentous revelation. "Christ, Greysen. That's ridiculously insane. I mean, awesome, but insane."

Greysen nodded, pinching the bridge of his nose. "The problem was... the synapses in our brains function in a way so that if you want to extract knowledge or memories, you can't just take what you want. There's always a price to pay. And I wasn't willing to take that chance, you know? After the merciless behavior Edrick exercised on some of my previous inventions, I couldn't go through that again. This could change the future of mankind!" He raised his hands in the air. "We would have a huge influx of knowledge and history! But it could also be very, very dangerous if fallen into the wrong hands."

Parker looked at Greysen, wide-eyed. "What are the odds of them actually developing this?"

Greysen merely met his gaze, silent.

Parker noticed a broken blood vessel in the white of his left eye. His lips were pressed into a thin line. "Holy shit," Parker concluded at the man's continued silence. "You think they have it already."

"This is why I think you need to go into hiding. They will come after you. Even if they don't need you to get to me, you know too much. Proven by that damned book I had you write." He stood and paced again. "I should have never brought you into this." He stared into Parker, his face drained of color.

Parker stood and held his hand out to Greysen's chest. "No. Don't do that now, c'mon. I chose to be involved just as much as you involved me. I wrote that book, so that others could learn from your experience. You have changed many people's lives for the better, including mine, okay?"

Greysen hung his head.

Parker clapped his hand on the side of Greysen's arm. "But... but what are you going to do, Greysen? You can't tell me you're going to go after Molly?"

Greysen scoffed and rubbed the back of his neck. "I mean, I'll be careful. I'll use my trusted connections. If she's alive and being held against her will or forced to do things, then I need to see if there's any possibility of righting this. I need to save her."

"But they only want you, right? I can help! I can track them down for you! I've already been in contact with Molly. I can play a double agent!"

"No. That's very nice of you, Parker. But this is not a game. Your efforts of *playing a double agent* could lead you to a bullet between your eyes." He lifted his grungy finger and pointed to Parker's forehead. Then, he looked him in the eyes. " You need to get away. Far away. You cannot win. You will not win. They are very powerful. This is my problem... this has always been my problem. It's time for me to deal with it, end it, once and for all. It's come to the point where I am tired of living in fear. "

Parker nodded. "I mean, I don't know how you've done it this entire time, honestly. Aside from making yourself believe that you deserve this."

They sat a moment in silence before Parker spoke again. "I need to get back to Noriana. Let her know I'm still alive after my street incident."

After such an intense discussion, both of them chuckled under their breaths at his comment.

"You did make a pretty terrible homeless person." Greysen smirked.

Parker laughed, before getting back to the matter at hand. "How will I get in contact with you again if I need to?"

"Leave it to me. I will get in contact with you if need be."

Parker wasn't entirely sure he fully understood the implications of that. He walked over to the single armchair in the room and picked up his crumpled hoodie. Slipping it over his arms and lifting the hood over his head. Before he headed for the door, he turned to Greysen. "Greysen, please be careful. I beg you." He leaned in and put his arms around Greysen for a hug. It was the first time he'd ever embraced the man. When he backed up, he thought he saw him overcome with emotion, his shoulders hunched and his eyes glistening.

"You too, kid." Greysen mumbled.

Parker reached for the door handle and then stopped. "Wait, how do I get out of here? I wasn't entirely conscious when we arrived."

Greysen stifled a small laugh as he composed himself. "We're located right above the Latin Quarter. Walk south and you'll begin to recognize things. Just don't go down any small side streets that look dark. It's dangerous."

Parker looked up at him with an eyebrow raised. "I'm sorry, tell me again where I can go where it *isn't* dangerous?"

"Touché."

TEN

Parker made it back through the questionable neighborhood with his hood up, head down, and hands in his pockets. Greysen had been right. Once he got through the first few turns moving south, he recognized the cozy, historic Latin Quarter neighborhood. It wove around Le Sacre Coeur, the highest point in Paris, and ultimately close to the L'Universite de Sorbonne dormitories. All his things he normally had with him, his phone, his bag with his laptop, and all the rest of it was back with Noriana, so he had no way of telling her he was coming. He hoped she was at the college, or else he'd have to wait there until she returned.

He knocked on her door.

A woman with a short, blonde-haired bob opened it. "Hello there," she answered in a British accent.

"You must be Nori's roommate?" he asked.

She smiled. "Yea, I'm Char. You must be Nori's man?" she asked.

He chuckled, trying to see past her into the small dorm room. "She here?"

She stepped back from the door to show him the empty room.
"She went to go turn in a paper to a professor. She should be back in a minute."

"Okay. I'll just, uhh, wait for her, yeah? I'll just wait out here."

"You big silly, you can come in!" She went into the room and left the door open. She hopped up onto her bed with her laptop and began clicking away at the keys.

"Uhh, thanks," he said awkwardly as he walked into the room. He didn't close the door. He had just sat down on Nori's bed, parallel with Charlotte's, when Noriana came through the door. Charlotte hadn't been kidding when she'd said Nori would be back in 'a minute'.

"Oh my God, Parker, you're alive!" Nori yelled, throwing her arms around him. "What happened?" She backed up and held his shoulders, looking him up and down. "What the hell happened? You okay?" She touched his face.

"You want me to leave, mate?" Charlotte's small voice rang out behind Noriana.

"Oh, Char! No, you're fine. We're going to take off. You can stay, thank you." She reached into her desk drawer and retrieved Parker's things. "Here, babe. We can talk on the walk."

He couldn't find a good time to talk in between all her words. "I'm great, Nori," he managed at last. "Had a pretty awful night, but..."

Noriana closed the dorm room door behind them and they began their trek across the campus and through the Latin Quarter. She cut him off, "Please tell me you found him."

He grabbed her hand as they walked, lacing his fingers through hers. "I found him."

"He's here still?" she whispered excitedly as she gripped his hand tighter.

He nodded.

"The news wasn't good, huh?" She lowered her voice.

"Nuh uh," he responded.

"We can talk when we get back to your hotel," she said.

He was grateful for that. She must have sensed his hesitation to speak in public. They rounded the corner and headed down some stairs and a metal arch over the entrance that read, "Metropolitan".

He twisted the key and pushed the door ajar, allowing Noriana to enter first. Everything in France seemed small compared to the space he was used to having in America. But he didn't need much here. Just a place to lay his head.

This room proved to be a little less hostile than the hotel he'd just come from with Greysen, with clean lines and modern decor. Everything looked like it was straight out of an Ikea catalogue. Fresh, clean lines. There was a massive window on one wall that allowed the dusky glow of the sun in through the sheer curtains. His hotel room was on the fifth floor, so he didn't need to worry about anybody seeing in his window.

"How did he take the news about Molly?" Noriana asked softly.

"He was happy, of course, to have it confirmed, but he already had an inkling that she was alive."

They spent the next few hours lying in bed and talking to each other as they stared up at the textured ceiling. He told her everything. About his night as a sorry homeless person and how he almost froze to death under that bridge before, just by chance, Greysen found him. Then he told her about the prostitute motel he'd woken up in and the fountain of doomed lovers, the roses, and the blueprints for the invention.

"I can't believe what I'm hearing," Nori muttered when he'd finished the whole story. "This is crazy. It's like we're in a sci-fi novel!" She propped herself up on her elbows, facing him in the bed. "There's a way to extract memories from us?"

"Yeah, but Greysen's plan for it was to help those that are old and about to pass on. So all their experiences and knowledge that took a lifetime to collect could be passed down in a more accurate way... a way that doesn't rely on word-of-mouth or memoir or people's sometimes-faulty memories. A way that insures all their experience and knowledge doesn't go to waste."

"That sounds really cool."

"But he hid the invention away because he didn't want it falling into the wrong hands and used for bad things. He's been burned in the past. And it effected the lives of so many people." He laid back on the pillow and reached his hands up to his head.

"Yeah..." she trailed off, slumping back down.

"So, I need to hide somewhere where nobody would suspect me to be," Parker said. "Because Edrick's men still seem to think I know where Greysen is. And now... well, now I kinda *do* know where Greysen is. And I don't want to be a liability for him. Also, I know too much." He turned onto his side, facing Noriana in the bed.

They lay together in silence a moment, and then her eyes grew wider with a realization.

"I know where you can go," she started. "My parents have a vacation home, a cabin, in an isolated area northeast of San Francisco. You could go there. Even if they've been watching you, they don't even know what my role is in this whole thing. I'm of no concern to them. So how would they suspect you'd be at my family's vacation home? It's a great spot to hide away."

"That's a great idea, babe." He smiled, tracing all the features on her face with his eyes. "I guess I outta go tomorrow," he said, staring off into the distance behind her. "And I feel like I just got back with you."

"Because you did." She sighed. "It's hard doing this long-distance thing, huh?" she asked.

"Harder than I thought, yeah. But it's always worth it when I get to be with you. It's like... if it wasn't for Greysen to begin with, leaving that note on my car that led me to the museum you worked at, I never would have met you. But also, if it weren't for Greysen, I wouldn't have to be on the run, leaving you again."

"You talk too much," she whispered, and then placed her hand on the bed in-between them to lean into him.

As she leaned in, he touched her cheek and kissed her on the lips. Soft at first, and then it gradually got rougher as he felt her tongue roll into his mouth.

"If this..." He kissed her again. "Is our last night for a long while..." He breathed in-between kisses. "Then let's make it a night to remember."

She pushed his hoodie off his shoulders, the sleeves catching on his wrists. He shook it off behind him, then put both palms on her hips.

As she ran her thin, long fingers through his hair, he reversed the fabric on her shirt and lifted it up. When he got to her neck, she assisted in pulling the shirt off over her head, tossing it to the floor.

"Parker..." she breathed.

He yanked his own shirt off and looked down at her breasts, cradled in her nude-lace bra. He stood up, and Noriana followed.

Without hesitation, she reached forward and pushed the button of his jeans out of the loop. She unzipped them and carefully pushed them off his hips. They fell to the floor, and he kicked them off his feet.

She reached down and pushed her own black yoga pants off, kicking them away as well. They stood in the golden light of the hotel room, observing each other's bodies in their underwear.

Parker was already astounded by her body, each and every curve more beautiful than the next. In the few moments his mind gave himself to think, he couldn't believe they were doing what they were doing. After all this time of being apart, and after what happened in the Bed and Breakfast last year, he thought it'd take them a lot longer to get here than it had. But he wasn't complaining, and he wasn't going to stop it. It just felt right to be here with her. In this room.

Nobody knew they were here.

Parker looked over his shoulder at the bathroom. He was lucky to have a sink and shower in his hotel room. The toilets were in a separate closet room down the hall and were shared, but the rest of a bathroom was actually connected to his room, thankfully.

He looked back at Noriana to see her smiling. "Do you wanna?" he asked, nodding to the shower. "It's been a long last two days."

She giggled. "Yes. I do."

He turned and went for the bathroom, Noriana behind him.

The floor tiles were cold on his bare feet. He pushed the glass door back. He leaned in and twisted the knob to the shower; a slight high-pitched scream of the pipes sounded before a gush of water rushed out.

Noriana's hands slinked around his hips from behind and he felt a kiss like fire on the side of his neck.

He turned from the shower to find her on her tip-toes, and he grabbed her close, pulling her to his bare chest. He unhooked her bra from behind the embrace, and felt her shoulder relax into him.

The water rushed behind him and sounded like a waterfall hitting rocks below. She kissed his neck again as he smoothed her hair. She backed up from him and slipped her arms out of the bra straps.

He watched as the bra fell to the floor between them and hit his toes. Inhaling, he felt the blushing heat rush to his face.

It'd been a while since he'd been with anyone like this. And he'd never been with someone he was so attracted to, someone so beautiful inside and out. The corner of her lips curved, and he knew what came next.

She reached for his light gray boxer briefs and pulled the elastic band down his legs. Her entire body moved down with his underwear, and she squatted on the ground, her face level with his crotch.

His muscles tightened, and he followed her every silent command, lifting each foot out of his boxers.

She tossed them aside and worked her way back to his face, brushing his bare body with her own. He reached for her panties, and she helped him get them off. Even before he fully got her feet free, she was shoving him into the shower, and then pounced onto him under the water.

They both yelled out at the shock of the ice-cold temperature as it splashed down over their heads.

"Shit, shit, shit!" Parker yelled, and Noriana began to laugh from her gut. Parker fumbled with the knob on the shower wall and discovered the cold and hot were opposite of what he was used to. He wasn't sure if this was a French thing or just the plumbing installed backwards.

Either way, after the initial shock of the chilling cold water, they were both laughing, and instantly the water turned warm, comforting their bodies once more.

"That was cra—" he began, when Noriana placed her hands on his shoulders and pushed him softly into the wall of the shower, kissing him on the mouth. He tenderly reciprocated and was instantly brought back to the moment. The warm, borderline-too-hot water soaked them, flowing over their bodies together in unison. The water rushed over his eyes and lashes, making them heavy, making him want to close them, but he just couldn't take his eyes off of her. Her glistening, wet body was enough to send him over the edge. He spun her around and heard her exhale in exasperation. He turned the tables on her and placed her against the wall, his hand on the back of her head to catch it from hitting. She closed her eyes, feeling him up and down with her hands. He grabbed her chin and kissed her.

"Nori—" he breathed.

She opened her eyes and looked into his.

"Can I—"

"Yes."

He pressed into her, and they melted into the glistening green tiles of the shower wall together.

ELEVEN

P arker leaned his head against the wall and peered out the oval window, overlooking the plane's wing.

Here I am again... on an airplane. He watched person after person waddle through the aisle and subconsciously judged each one. One of these lucky people would get to be his seat neighbor for the next half a day while they flew over the ocean to San Francisco.

He found it much harder to be on the airplane this time, far more than all the others. This time was different. He was in hiding. Running from someone, someone capable of horrible things.

And last night he'd had the time of his life with Noriana. He felt a true connection with her. For almost the first time in their relationship, she'd been vulnerable with him. He'd never experienced that level with her and assumed it didn't come out too often.

He hadn't wanted to leave her that next morning. He didn't want to leave her, ever. What was worse was that he wasn't sure when would be the next time he would see her.

She'd told him all the things he needed to know to get to the cabin. He was going to land in San Francisco and get picked up by her parents. That, in itself, was nerve-racking. Meeting the girlfriend's parents for the first time. On their turf. *Without* the girlfriend.

She'd assured him over and over that they were nice, and he'd be fine, but still. And under these circumstances, they probably thought he was running from the law for some reason, like an escaped convict. That would make for some good small talk.

As these thoughts circulated around his mind, a girl in her early twenties wearing yoga clothes stopped at the end of his aisle and placed her backpack in the overhead bin before twisting her body into his row of seats.

He lifted his head from the window and looked forward, not wanting to look directly at her. *If I look at her, she will think I'm judging her as she chooses her seat next to me. Thank God she's not a hairy man who takes up two seats. Oh my God, who's going to get the arm rest? Wait! I am judging her!*

He looked.

She was a short blonde, with black, square-rimmed glasses. She smiled at him as she sat in the seat next to him, fumbling with her seat belt.

Parker nodded in hello, and laid his head back on the window. *Act... natural,* he thought, mentally kicking himself again for being the most awkward person on the face of planet Earth.

"Are you going to need that?" she asked.

"Huh?" He lifted his head and looked all around.

She giggled. "That magazine?" She nodded to his seat-back pocket. "Are you going to need it?" she asked again.

He shook his head. "Uhh, you can have it. Sorry." He reached forward and grabbed the magazine, handing it to her. He hesitated and then asked, "Are you American?" All signs pointed to yes, but he was still used to asking when somebody spoke to him in English. And they hadn't lifted off the ground yet.

"Yes, I am. Are you?"

"It's not that obvious, huh?" he joked.

She laughed again. "Are you going home? Do you live in San Fran?"

He shook his head. "No, I'm just going there for vacation." He cleared his throat. *Some sorry excuse of a vacation.*

"Oh, you live in Paris, then?"

115

"Actually no. Heh!" A thought crossed his mind that perhaps he should be careful how much he told this girl. They'd just met. And he was already telling her everything about his life. Hadn't he learned anything? "My girlfriend is in Paris right now for school, and I'm going to San Francisco to visit one of my buddies before I head back home. Are you going home?" *Nice one! That sounded convincing enough. I could have buddies.*

"Yeah, I live in the bay area. I was actually just meeting up with my Dad who takes regular business trips to Paris. He let me stay with him for a week. I teach yoga in the city."

"Wow, that's awesome!" he responded. *Good. I was able to work into the conversation that I have a girlfriend. Did she catch that? That way she won't think I'm creeping on her when we talk.*

Parker was generally a pretty social guy, who obviously had no problems talking with strangers when given the opportunity. But the night before he'd gotten very little sleep, for reasons he wasn't complaining about, so he figured it'd be smart to sleep on the airplane back to the States. "I'm Parker, by the way," he said and turned to shake her hand. *Do people still shake hands in situations like this?*

She nodded, smiled, and shook his hand.
Her hand felt dainty and cold in his own.

"My name's Jackie. I'll leave you be. I'm going to read for a while." She leaned back in her chair.

"Yeah, thanks."

"Let me know if you need anything."

"Huh?" He nerves began to stir.

"To get out of the aisle or something."

"Ah, right. Okay, thanks." He smiled, then melted into the seat. She was super nice. He'd gotten lucky. He turned his body toward the window and pulled the shade down to lean his head against it once more. He put his headphones on and was out before the airplane finished taxiing.

He woke up because his music stopped. The flight attendant cracked onto the loud speaker to tell them they were making their descent into Chicago to switch planes. He wiped a bit of drool from his mouth and turned to see Jackie stirring as well.

"Good morning, sleepy head," she joked to Parker.

Suddenly he felt self-conscious.

"You were out the whole time! Even missed the dinner cart!"

He laughed. "Yeah I was exhausted. It's alright. Is this one of those where we wait in the plane while they refuel and then we continue?" He'd been on so many of these things that he couldn't remember what his ticket said.

"No, I think we switch planes," she responded, looking back and forth, up and down the aisle.

Parker forgot that the free Wi-Fi they offered on the plane allowed him to send and receive messages. He leaned forward and pulled his cell phone out of the front pocket of his backpack under the seat in front of him. He had several messages, one of which was from Noriana.

It said her parents could no longer pick him up at the airport, but if he could find a way to get to their house, they would be able to take him out to the cabin. That wasn't too bad. He'd weathered public transportation before.

"Hey Jackie?" he asked.

She turned to him. "Hm?"

"I just found out my ride from the airport can't come anymore. Can you tell me which route to take with public transportation that's the easiest?" he asked.

"Yeah, sure thing! We've got all the time in the world before we land."

He realized just then that maybe he could have asked Nori how to do this. Then he felt a pang of guilt in the pit of his stomach. Was he cheating on Noriana by asking another girl how to get somewhere?

Don't be ridiculous. That's crazy thinking. Nori isn't that kind of girl. And what if Jackie was a sixty-year-old man and not a hot, blonde, twenty-something? Oh my god, she's hot?

When they landed in San Francisco and made their way out of the plane and into the airport, Parker turned to Jackie before she took off. "Hey, thanks for all your help, Jackie!"

She smiled and pulled out a piece of paper, scrawling something down on it. "Here, Parker. If you need any more help, give me a call."

He took the paper and shoved it into his jeans, nodding in thanks, and then took off in the other direction.

Jackie was a nice person and he appreciated the gesture. Though he'd probably never call her. "Take the F line..." he whispered to himself.

He jumped off the street car and walked past the theatre that was famous for so many triumphs for gay rights. Down at the bottom of a long, steep street, he turned the corner, and pulled his phone out one more time to look at the address. "Noe Valley..." he whispered as he turned up their street.

He studied the different houses as he walked through the neighborhood. They were all stacked high to maximize space, as opposed to what he was used to in Kansas City; houses that had spacious yards, and ranch-style homes. These houses were right next to each other, with maybe something that could be considered an alley way in-between them.

He came up to a tan house with white trim and very well-manicured bushes and flowers lining the walk.

This was it.

He took a massive breath into his lungs and walked up to the door.

After he knocked and stood awkwardly on the deck, a woman opened the door.

She had dark brown hair that was held up in a back-hair clip. This was definitely the right house. The woman was a spitting image of Noriana, though twenty or so years older, of course.

"Mrs. Page?" he asked.

She came across the threshold and threw her arms around him, which startled him, but he embraced her in return. She backed up and shook his shoulders. "You must be Parker!" she said happily. "Come in! Please come in!"

He laughed sheepishly and picked up his backpack, walking into the house.

It was laid out just the way it looked from the outside. Long and skinny, with bedrooms on the left-hand side. Down the hall, it opened up to an eat-in living and kitchen area. There was no upstairs, and Parker realized that this one house was separated into four different people's houses in one building, a fourplex. And though it was small, it still felt like enough space, especially if it was just Noriana's mom and dad.

"Thank you for making me feel so welcomed!" He told her as he followed her into the family room.

Noriana's dad was sitting on the couch, watching television.

Parker immediately walked up to him and put out his hand to shake. Her father seemed impressed and he stood, shaking Parker's hand with a firm grip. "Nice to meet you, Parker, you can call me Jack."

"Yeah, yeah," Nori's mom said, "and none of this Mrs. Page nonsense. I'm Anya. Can I get you a drink?" she asked.

"Yeah that'd be great. Thank you. Just water's fine."

"We have Coke. Do you want a Coke?"

"Yeah sure." He placed his bag down on the ground and sat in the one other armchair in the room, off the couch. "It's kind of weird meeting you guys without Nori here." He laughed nervously.

Jack had CNN playing on the television in front of them. They were covering a story on the vandalization of churches in Eastern Europe.

As Anya was busy clanking dishes in the kitchen, Jack turned to Parker.

Parker gulped. His heart began to race a little.

"So what'd you do?" Jack asked.

"Whoa, okay, just right out of the gate there." His voice was higher-pitched than normal.

Jack's expression was amused, which lightened the mood a little and made Parker feel a little better. "You're dating my daughter," he stated.

"Yes, yeah that's true." Parker smiled.

"She doesn't ask me to hide her boyfriends away at our vacation cabin very often."

"Boyfriends? Like with an s on the end there?"

Jack chuckled. "I like you," he said calmly. "But no, really, what kind of mess are you in?"

Now was the time to either be honest, or not. Since he'd been honest with Noriana, and he didn't know what she'd shared with her parents, he'd better be honest with them, too.

122

"Uhhh, well, I wrote a book."

"I *read* your book."

"You did!?"

They both laughed.

"Well thank you," Parker continued. "Yeah, I wrote a book that I marketed as fiction... and there are some bad people out there who think it's true, so now they are after me." If he was going to be honest about this mess, then it was going to be to the father of the girl he was dating. After all, they were helping him. They deserved to know what they were getting into as well.

"*Is* it fiction?" Jack asked.

Parker hesitated and looked the man in the eye.

"You don't have to tell me. It's okay." He nodded.

Anya came over at that moment and handed them both their iced drinks, then sat on the couch next to Jack.

"We're gonna help you, Parker. Because we love our daughter." He smiled.

"What are you guys chatting about?" Anya asked.

Parker looked at Jack.

"Oh, Jack, are you teasing the boy?" She hit her husband on the side of the arm.

He shrugged. "After we finish our drinks," he said to Parker, "we're going to take off. I was just going to have Anya stay here while I take you out there. It's about a three-hour drive, just North of Yosemite. Anya's working from home today, so she'll be more productive without us here anyhow."

"I wish you could stay longer, Parker," Anya said. "But we understand the circumstances. And we're happy to be here for you." She smiled.

Parker sipped the Coke. It felt good fizzing down his throat. "Thank you guys so much for your hospitality. I can see where Noriana got her great personality. You guys have no idea how much I appreciate this."

"Alright, hopeless romantic, grab your bag." Jack stood up, finished his drink, and walked around to place his glass on the counter.

"I'll be back, sweetheart." He leaned down and kissed his wife.

Parker scrambled for his bag.

TWELVE

Aside from the awkward, *I'm in the car with my girlfriend's father whom I just met* situation, the drive was beautiful.

Parker hadn't realized California was so lush. There were rolling hills of green that dropped off from the road, and no guard rail to protect them from plunging into the hilly oblivion.

"So, how's Nori doing?" Jack asked as they cruised down the two-lane highway through the California countryside.

"She's great. Back into the swing of things at school." A vision flashed across his mind of the last time he'd seen her, in bed with him, her warm body tucked into his.

"Are you in school?" Jack asked.

"Uhh, no. I went for a bachelor's back in Kansas City. University of Central Missouri. But I... stopped going. I never thought it'd benefit me to go to school for what I want to do. Which is write."

"How'd you meet Nori then if you didn't meet at school?" he asked.

"Uh, it's a funny story actually," Parker chuckled. "I met her while she was giving a tour at the Museum of Modern Art in Paris. I heard her voice. I hit a dead end in my job and went to Paris alone to finish my novel."

"That's responsible," Jack said, sarcasm dripping off his words.

Parker laughed. He was finally beginning to loosen up a bit and understand Noriana's dad's humor. "Yeah well, we saw how it turned out, right?"

Now it was Jack's turn to laugh. "You can hold your own, you know that?"

"I try, I try."

They both laughed together.

"Anyway..." Parker continued, "back to telling you how I first met your daughter—"

Jack chuckled again.

"I was writing on a bench in the museum and I heard her voice. I was drawn to it, so I tried to sneak in to her tour and she kicked me out. Said all the other people paid for it and I had to go down and buy a ticket if I wanted to listen in. So I went and bought a ticket."

126

"Well, she seems to have really taken a liking to you. I told her it'd never work out with the long-distance you guys have. But what twenty-four-year-old is going to listen to her father? I want her to succeed, but she didn't listen to me when I told her there are several museums in San Francisco that she could work at, either. She had to go all the way across the world to find one." He lifted his hands from the wheel in a shrug, and then took the wheel once more.

Parker looked out the window and back to him. "I understand. You're her dad. You want to make sure she's safe. My mom was the same way when I dropped everything to fly to Paris. Apart from it being so cliché, she was worried about me functioning on my own. Well, I'm an adult and I handled it..." A flash of everything that had happened to him since he'd stepped foot in Charles de Gaulle the year prior played in his mind. *Yeah right, handled it? Ha!*

Jack turned onto a side road. The path was much more rugged than the paved highway, but perhaps that's why he drove a Subaru Outback.

The rest of the trip, Parker bounced in the passenger seat, at the mercy of the uneven road, in silence. Jack played a Bob Dylan through the car stereo.

"Now, Anya bought you some groceries before you got to our house," Jack said suddenly, "so those are in coolers in the back. We just need to take them in once we get there. And I'll come back to check on you in about five days. You should have all the stuff you need in the cabin. There's more wood out back in a pile if you need more heat in the fireplace."

Parker could not express the level of gratitude he felt for Noriana's family, taking care of him like this. But he would try. "Thank you, Jack, so much. Seriously. You don't even know me, and you and Anya have done nothing but treat me like I'm your own son. I really appreciate this, so much."

"Well, like I told you earlier, we love our daughter. This is for her."

Parker saw a hint of a smile on his lips.

"One other thing," Jack started. "Your phone is pretty much obsolete out here." He nodded to the smart phone laying in Parker's lap. "There's absolutely no service. You won't be able to receive calls or messages, nor send them."

"Okay..." This made his feel wary. It instantly gave him the feeling of isolation, and he wasn't even in the cabin in the middle of nowhere alone yet. Isolation matched right up there with the cousin of paranoia.

What if something happened while he was there to put him in danger? *Oh my God, what could happen? What would I do? I couldn't call anyone. I could run, but where? I don't know where I am!* He realized then, his dependency on technology. It ran deep. "Well... what if something happens and I need help?" he asked Jack. The realization of the matter became even more real when he voiced it out loud.

"Do what people did before cell phones were invented," Jack teased, as he looked over at Parker. He must have realized then that Parker was being completely serious. "Damn, you really are in trouble, huh? We have a satellite phone in the cabin for emergencies. We've never had to use it, but I can show you how to work it."

Parker didn't answer, but just stared straight ahead, holding onto the door to stabilize himself from bouncing all over the place as they made their way closer to the cabin. The further they drove, Parker began to notice patches of snow and ice here and there, until the entire ground was covered with it.

It was freezing cold. He wasn't prepared for this. Of course, he had *some* winter-appropriate things packed, since he'd just come prepared for a winter in Paris.

"Look," Jack began. "You're going to this cabin to get away from everything, yeah? Nobody but my daughter and wife and I know you are coming here. You haven't told anybody, right?"

Parker shook his head. "No, I haven't. Not even my own family," he said quietly, which brought a bunch of other thoughts into his mind.

"Well there you have it! Nobody knows you will be here, and you'll be fine. Just get your notebook out and write another novel while you're by yourself," Jack finished.

Parker smiled. "You're a great guy, Jack."

"You are, too, from what Noriana's told us," Jack reciprocated, to Parker's relief. He hadn't been sure what Nori's parents would really think of him, given this situation. But it seemed he must be doing something right...

They sat for the next while in quiet as Parker mulled over his own thoughts.

THIRTEEN

Parker's eyelids grew heavy behind the windshield. The sun hung low in the sky. It carried an orange hue as it peeked just below the horizon, casting long shadows of the birch wood trees as they drove.

"This cabin means a lot to our family," Jack spoke again, lowly.

Parker looked over at him, rubbing at his eyes.

"We used to come here all the time when Nori was just a little girl. Anya and I had a rough ride for a while, and we bought this place to rekindle our love. It worked. Anya is the best woman who ever lived, and Noriana is our prize. We've had such great memories staying at this cabin. I hope it brings you as much solace as it has for our family." He turned up an even narrower road.

Parker suspected it to be the driveway. Sure enough, just around the bend, a very small log cabin sat at the end. The jeep plowed through the snow that blanketed the road, now covering it completely.

Jack pulled up next to the side of the cabin, as close as he could get. He put the car in park and pulled the key to the place off his key ring, handing it over to Parker. Then he got out and went around to the back of the jeep.

Parker followed him with his backpack on.

They grabbed the cooler and reusable grocery bags, loading up their arms, and staggered through the snow to the door. Parker grabbed the single key and slipped it into the lock, pushing the door forward.

The musty smell of cedar escaped outside, and Parker allowed Jack to go in first, looking back and forth into the trees before going in himself and closing the door behind them.

They set all the groceries up on the counter.

"Alright, bud," Jack said. "You've got full power, electricity and running water. It's a one-bedroom place, so the bedroom is down there and the bathroom just adjacent to it. Running fridge here for all your groceries, and like I said, please use the fireplace for heat."

"Do you have fire starter logs or something to get it going?" Parker asked, trying to keep up with all the instructions.

"In the kitchen drawer next to the sink, you've got some starters and a couple of lighters," Jack answered. "In the event that you lose power—the snow can get pretty heavy up here—there are candles in the closet, and of course the fireplace as well. And I will be back up here in five days."

Parker nodded, taking in everything he was saying. An overwhelming dread overcame him. He didn't want Jack, his girlfriend's dad, to leave him here. He didn't want to be alone. Part of it was that he was a social guy, and he didn't want to have to face himself in this cabin alone. He went around and sat on the coach apprehensively, staring into the grate of the fireplace.

"Hey, man..." Jack walked over to him and placed his hand on Parker's shoulder. "I'll be back here in five days. You'll be alright."

Parker nodded and tried to pull himself together. "Yeah, I'll be okay."

Jack hesitated. "Hey, come here," he said, turning from the sitting area and walking back towards the bedroom.

That seemed a bit weird to Parker. *Alright,* he thought. *I'll follow him to the bedroom*, he joked in his head. He walked down the narrow hall into a bedroom that had only a full-sized bed, and that was pretty much it.

Jack was crouched down at the end of the bed. "This," he said, with a black box opened in front of him, "is my forty-two revolver. Have you ever shot a gun before?" He looked up at Parker with his eyebrow raised.

Parker shook his head no.

"Oh geeze," Jack said under his breath. "Pull back the hammer, release, and pull the trigger, okay?"

Parker nodded, his muscles tensed.

"Repeat it back to me, okay? Here, feel it." He handed Parker the gun.

It was heavier than Parker had expected, cold metal. He felt up the smooth barrel and placed both hands on it, his finger on the trigger. "Pull back, release, and pull trigger," he said quietly.

"Yeah. It also has a safety, there." He pointed it out to Parker and demonstrated how to take it off and put it back on. "Now in the event you're in trouble— this is yours," Jack said.

Parker nodded, handing him back the gun.

Jack put it into the case and closed it, shoving it under the bed. "It's usually locked, but I'm going to leave it unlocked for easy access. I hope you don't need to use it. Be sure, okay?

Don't pull it out if a squirrel is patting at your window. Be sure. Be safe."

Parker nodded vigorously.

Jack stood back up. "Satellite phone." He pointed to the hallway, as if he'd just remembered the brief mention of it in the car.

Parker followed him back out.

Jack went to the front closet and pulled down the satellite phone. It was orange and black and looked like a clunky walkie-talkie. "It's already fully charged. So you're good to go. Just call 911 if you need help. Though don't expect anyone to be able to get out here quickly, especially in this weather."

Parker nodded and watched him put the phone back and close the closet door. His mind was already beginning to go into fight or flight mode.

"I'm gonna take off. You'll be alright." He clapped Parker on the shoulder again.

"Jack—" Parker started.

Jack turned to him.

"I want to give you my parents' number. If you come back in five days and something's happened to me, I want you to be the one that calls them. Please."

Jack nodded. "Nothing's going to happen to you, Parker, but I'll take your folks' number."

135

Parker turned to the fridge and ripped off a piece of paper from the magnetic tablet hanging there. He took a pen from the counter, scrawled down his mom's number, and handed it to Jack. Then, he advanced forward and threw his arms around Jack.

The man closed his own arms around Parker in an embrace. "Ah, come now. Anya's the hugging type, not me. You take care, alright?" And just like that, he was gone out the door.

Parker watched him from the window as he swerved the car up the makeshift driveway in the snow, and out of sight.

Parker was alone now.

Complete and utter isolation.

And just like clockwork, large fluffy snowflakes began to fall from the sky. A chill slinked across his shoulders. The snow would fall and fill in the tire tracks as if nobody had driven there at all.

And Parker would be alone.

In the cabin.

With nothing but the sound of the cardinals in the birch trees outside.

FOURTEEN

A few hours had passed since Jack had left. Parker was already beginning to feel antsy. He'd spent his time so far checking out the cabin and putting away the groceries that Noriana's parents had gotten for him.

"Oh my God, thank you! They really do love me." He pulled the packet of chocolate sandwich cookies from the bag. The rest consisted of some easy-to-prepare meals, cups of noodles, hummus and chips, stuff to make sandwiches, and a four-pack of Izzie's clementine sparkling water in glass bottles.

He was set.

He sighed and looked around the cabin.

"It's only five days till I get some information about civilization again," he told himself out loud. However, it'd only been one day that he'd posed as a homeless person, and he knew well enough what had happened then. *One* day. Now, he had five to endure. Though of course the situations were different. Here, he had food, a bathroom, and a warm bed to sleep in at the end of the day.

He went back into the bedroom to grab his notebook out of his backpack. When he stepped in the room and unzipped the bag, he remembered the conversation he'd had with Jack in this room.

He stopped fumbling in the bag and went to the end of the bed. He stopped a moment, and then knelt down and pulled the black box out from under the bed. When he opened the box and looked down at the black gun, his heart raced.

Taking the gun out and feeling the weight of it in his hands, he shoved it into the back waistband of his pants.

Then, he whipped around and yanked the gun out, pointing it at the wall. "Put em uuuup!" he yelled. He looked down at the gun in his hands again. "Damn, I'm cool," he whispered.

Then he kicked the box back under the bed, took the gun and his laptop, and went into the main room.

He went over to the couch and set his laptop down with the gun next to it, and then looked up at the fireplace.

It was already set up inside, with logs carefully stacked and a fire starter underneath. He took the long lighter that sat on the top of the mantle and clicked the light underneath the logs. Sure enough, the fire blazed into the chimney.

He set the lighter down where he got it and backed up to the couch, sitting down with the laptop on his lap, and the gun sitting next to him.

The crackling of the fire brought him out of the real world and into his writing world, somewhere he loved to be, and somewhere that had been neglected for near too long.

He ran. As fast as his legs would go. His lungs felt small, as if they were collapsing and buckling under him as he ran through the forest. Raging, barking dogs were just at his heels, their mouths snarling and drooling, sharp teeth flashing. His peripheral vision blacked out around the edges and he put his hands out to feel for any trees that he may pass.

Gasping for air, he felt his legs giving out.

"Shit! No!" he screamed. "Just a little further! Push it!" he spoke through gritted teeth and pained breaths. His foot caught in a root and he plunged to the ground. He remembered thinking, *This is it. This is the end.*

Parker jolted awake. His skin was damp with sweat, and his heart rate was through the roof. He gained consciousness of his surroundings.

The cabin. The fire was still dancing shadows off the walls and wooden floor before him. It was pitch black outside. He was still here, and still very much alone.

"I fell asleep," he said aloud, in hopes to feel better. He shut his laptop and walked to the kitchen. Standing in front of the sink, he splashed his face with cool water from the faucet.

He looked at the clock on the microwave. It was 2am.

He hadn't even made it through the first night yet. "Alright, the first night is the hardest." He zombied towards the bedroom, when something clicked in his mind.

The gun... He hurried back to the couch and grabbed it. The fire was only embers now, so he wouldn't need to put it out before moving to the bed. It would die out on its own.

140

He turned from the couch and began to head back to the bedroom when something caught his eye. He turned to the window.

"What?" He froze in his tracks. Unless his eyes were failing him, he'd thought he saw a light outside. But there was nothing else around this place for miles. Nothing. There would be nothing out here to produce a light.

He slowly walked over to the window and peered around the curtain. It was pitch black. The cabin didn't even have an outside light.

"I saw a light!" he yelled out. Parker let out a hard sigh and ripped the curtains closed. *What are the chances somebody's out there?*

His muscles tightened, and he realized he had gripped so tightly on the gun that the metal was cutting into the side of his thumb. He yanked his hand out and shook it.

You're tired. You probably saw a flash of an animal's eyes or something.

As if a coyote or other nocturnal animal in the woods outside of Yosemite National Park would be safer than something else that could produce that flash of light.

With the gun in hand, he stumbled back to the bedroom.

FIFTEEN

Parker woke up the next morning and stayed laying in the bed, looking up at the ceiling. He peered out the window of the bedroom to see that the sun was fully high in the sky now, and the snow had stopped. He felt bitter freezing down to the bone, and bundled the blankets to his neck, turning in the bed and curling up his feet.

"This damn cabin would be much better if Nori was here with me to share it," he said to himself, looking over at his phone on the end table. Even though he knew the service wouldn't work, he kept it close by. It was a security blanket. He didn't like the idea of this, but it was a given fact.

Having his phone close by just made him feel falsely secure. It was his answer for everything. He could look up anything he was confused about, call someone in need of help, look up the weather, everything. Right in the palm of his hand. And to be completely cut off from that was killing him. Though in some ways, he supposed he found it relaxing, as if he was cleansing himself of the technology that so often took control in his life. But when he thought about it more, that would only be effective if he had made the *choice* to shut it off. In this case, he had no control over whether or not he would get service, and it was during a time he needed it the most.

Was it really smart to hide himself in such a remote location with no help for miles? Wouldn't he have been safer had he stayed in the open public, with many witnesses to see if something was going to happen to him?

He also had no idea what he was up against. He knew very little. Apart from the stories he'd heard from Greysen about his experience with this man Edrick and his crew, whom he wasn't even sure who they consisted of, he knew nothing about them or what they were capable of. Perhaps that's where the nightmare with the dogs chasing him in the woods came from. The fact that Greysen had gone through those very experiences. And because Parker had written those stories, he felt like he had lived through the emotions of the experiences as well, even if he hadn't.

The thought of Greysen's invention came to mind. How was it even possible to harness a human's thoughts, memories, and knowledge? What were the possible consequences Greysen had warned about?

He lifted his phone from the end table and saw that it was almost noon.

Man, I slept a long time. Must have really needed it.

The only thing that brought him out of the warm bed was the grumbling of his stomach. He walked to the kitchen and opened the fridge, taking out the milk. Anya had bought him cereal. His favorite too. Count Chocula. He wondered if Noriana had told her and he laughed in spite of it. He poured up a bowl and walked back into the family room. As he ate, shriveled up on the couch, he thought about how he wanted to start another fire. It was cold in the cabin, and the only source of heat besides layering up was to keep feeding the fireplace that lumber. The cabin was small enough that once a good fire got going, it warmed up the whole place.

He finished his bowl and put it in the sink. Then walked to the door.

He needed to go out around back and get more wood if he was going to start a fire again.

145

He searched around the cabin and found a pair of boots in the front closet. They must have been Jack's, because they were a little big for him, but they would be better than getting his shoes soaked with wet, cold snow.

He pulled the tan snow boots onto his feet and opened the front door. A rush of cold blew into the cabin, and he instantly regretted not grabbing a coat. His t-shirt and red plaid fleece pajama pants were not going to cut it. Though he wouldn't be outside for very long. He trekked through the snow, around to the side of the cabin.

When he took a moment to notice his surroundings, he realized just how peaceful everything was. The smell of the fresh fallen snow. The white trunks of the naked birch trees. Only the bitterness of his nose and the sting in his nostrils from the freezing air that kept him moving. He rounded the back of the cabin and saw the stack of wood that Jack had told him about, laying in a metal rack away from the house.

He began to stack up the wood in his arms, as much as he could carry so he didn't have to come back out here for a while. Just as he turned from the woodpile, he saw some tracks in the snow by the tree line.

That must be the animal prints from last night, he thought as curiosity got the best of him. With the stack of wood in hand, he pushed through the snow and made his way to the tracks. As he came upon them, he followed the line across the snow. They disappeared into the trees.

They weren't coyote or wolf or dog. They weren't raccoon. They weren't elk.

They were human.

A rush of panic flooded Parker's body. He turned from the tracks and ran back toward the cabin. The thickness of the snow slowed him down immensely, and his feet pushed the snow into a wall pile that tripped him in his step. He fell forward, the wood flying from his arms, crashing to the ground.

He yelled out, and the snow seeped right into his fleece pants.

His breath came heavily as he pushed himself up in the snow. He collected the wood as fast as he could and looked all around him.

Someone was there with him. Or at least, they had been. That light he'd seen last night wasn't a *something*, it was a *someone*.

As soon as he got back into the cabin, he slammed the door shut, dropped the logs of wood at his feet, and locked the door with his raw fingers. His fingers and hands were numb.

147

He ran back to the bedroom and fumbled around the bed for the gun. Why hadn't he brought it with him? Retrieving it, he looked out all the windows of the cabin, searching the perimeter for any signs of life.

He located the satellite phone, and then tried to dial out. He called Noriana. Nothing. He tried his parents. Nothing. He realized then he'd never gotten Jack or Anya's number.

He thought about calling 911, but what would he say? He saw footprints? He's not alone when he was supposed to be alone? Nothing had happened just yet. But of course when things *were* happening, it would be too late to call for help.

He remembered when Greysen was in trouble, Greysen couldn't have contacted the police even if he'd wanted to all those years ago, because he had been a wanted man for kidnapping a little girl. Even though Corin had gone with him by choice, she was still a minor.

But even if Parker was in great danger and did try and call the police, it'd be hours before anyone could even get to him. By then, it might just be too late.

He went into the bedroom and picked up his cell phone. No service, to be expected. Having both phones was absolutely no use to him.

Frustration built up inside. He felt trapped. Claustrophobic.

He chucked the satellite phone onto the bed, and looked down at his cell phone. Then, he grabbed his phone and threw it with all his strength at the opposite wall. Right upon impact, the screen shattered into thousands of lines cracked across the screen.

That had helped get his anger out a little bit. He turned to his bag and grabbed out a pair of jeans, changing from his wet fleece pants into jeans, and then shoved the gun back into his waistband.

He regretfully grabbed his phone off the floor.

He went back into the main room and grabbed some of the wood to stack it up in the grate. He grabbed the lighter on the mantle and started the dying embers back up into a blazing fire.

With his phone, he walked to the bathroom. He stood in front of the toilet and chucked the phone into the water.

There. Now his phone was gone and with that, any sense of having a safety net to the outside world.

There was nothing left to do but sit there and wait for them to come, whoever they were. They were going to get him whether he was prepared or not, so he might as well be prepared.

He went back to the family room, sat on the ground in front of the fire and kicked his feet up on the brick. The flames licked the air above and toasted the bottom of his numb feet. The bitter wind whistled outside.

SIXTEEN

P arker laid down in front of the fireplace on the floor of the cabin, resting his eyes on the ceiling in a daze. The gun lay next to him. It had only been a few hours since he'd seen the tracks.

There was a knock.

On the door. Of the cabin Parker was currently in.

At first, he thought he was imagining it just like everything else. Some sort of self-prophecy. He sat up.

When it happened again, a knock that happened three or four times, he knew it was real.

Maybe Jack had come back to check on him? *No. It isn't Jack.* He'd said he wasn't coming back for another four more days.

Parker's muscles tensed. There were no windows by the front door, or else he'd try and see if he could tell who it was.

He flinched when the person knocked again, more aggressively this time.

Shit! He grabbed the gun and secured it back in his pants. Then, he stood from the floor and walked to the door, reaching slowly for the doorknob. He failed to steady his hand as he tried to unlock the deadbolt. He closed his eyes briefly and took a deep breath. Then twisted the deadbolt lock. The door pulled back, letting a gust of bitter cold air waft into the warm cabin.

"I didn't think you were going to answer!" she yelled, her eyes watery from the cold.

Parker crossed his arms over his chest as he looked around for a vehicle. He didn't know what to think as he looked out the doorframe of the isolated cabin, in the middle of nowhere, at Molly.

His first instinct was skepticism. "How did you get here?" he asked.

"I parked just up the road. It was near impossible getting here in the storm."

"No. How did you know I was here, Molly?" He turned his head and narrowed his eyes.

"We've plenty to talk about. Are you going to invite me in? It's freakin' cold."

"No. I want an answer."

"I tracked your phone."

Parker's intuition told him to get back in the cabin, so he backed up over the threshold and reached for the door. He tried to push it shut, but she was quicker.

She plunged forward and grabbed the wood, stuffing her boot into the crack before he could close it. "I said. Let me in." Her voice was colder than the wind that stung his lungs as he breathed.

It startled him enough to let go of the door.

She opened it and pushed her way in.

He spun around quickly so she couldn't see the gun in the back of his pants. "Are you alone?" he asked warily, watching her barge into the kitchen.

"Yeah. Who would be with me?" she asked, looking over to the fireplace.

He shrugged. "What are you looking for?" he asked quietly as her eyes searched around the cabin. He still didn't close the door.

"C'mon Parker, where is he?" she asked calmly.

"Greysen isn't here. Why did you track my phone?" He tried to keep his cool, but the entirety of the situation gave him a bitter taste in his mouth. Something wasn't right. "I told you I didn't know where he was!"

"But you're lying!" she said, raising her voice again. "When we ate breakfast together, I put a tracker in your phone when you went to get that coffee for your girlfriend. Just recently, the tracker went dead." She kept her golden eyes pinned on him. "You gonna close that door?" She held her hands up, as if to show she didn't have anything to harm him with.

Without taking his eyes off her, he slammed the door, snow falling from the roof in front of the window and piling below.

"Yeah, it went dead because I threw my phone in the toilet." He nodded over to the bathroom.

Molly took it upon herself to walk out of the kitchen and over to the hearth. She sat down on the couch.

Parker didn't move from his spot. He couldn't. He didn't want her to see the nerves building up inside him. He was still confused as to why she was here, and didn't have any way of asking for help.

"Why did you do that?" she asked.

Should I tell her the real reason? "I was mad that it wasn't of any assistance to me," he stated. That was *technically* the truth. "You gonna tell me why you tracked me to begin with, Molly? I deserve to know."

She heaved a sigh and sank back into the couch. "I thought... I thought you'd lead me to Greysen. I followed your trace all the way to Paris, and then here... I thought maybe you'd picked him up there and then came to this cabin to hide out. Thought you'd bring me to him. And when the signal went dark, I had to go to its last location." She stared into the flames as they reflected in her eyes.

Parker scoffed and shook his head. "Molly! Don't you think if Greysen wanted to see you, he would come to you?"

He saw her jaw clench, but pressed on. "I went to Paris to be with my girlfriend at her University before her classes started again after Christmas break! Didn't you see I was in the University de Sorbonne?" He hoped she wasn't good at telling if somebody was lying or not.

She didn't answer.

"So, he's not in the cabin, huh?" Her voice was rough now, harsh. She stood up from the couch and made her way down the hall. She smashed open the door to the bathroom, slamming it against the wall. Next came the bedroom.

Parker ran down the hall after her, reaching behind him for the gun.

155

"Molly! You leave me no choice!" He pointed the gun at her in the bedroom, trying to keep his hands steady under the weight of it, so she couldn't see his fear.

She turned, then pursed her lips at the sight of the weapon.

"Get the fuck out of my cabin," he said. "*Now.*"

She put her hands up.

He backed out and down the hall, and she followed him with her hands up.

"I didn't want to have to do this, Parker," she whispered, her eyes stark.

"Huh?" he asked.

She turned and looked at the door of the cabin. Before he had a moment to react, it busted open, hanging off the hinges, and two men barged in.

Pull back, blah blah, release... He recounted Jack's words on how to use the gun and pulled the trigger. The weapon fired, deafening, the recoil shocking up Parker's arms. The bullet ricocheted off the frame of the door. He'd missed the men by a mile.

One of them yelled, "Gun!"

Parker was largely outnumbered. He could not win.

156

His own father's words came rushing into his head in that moment. *Never start a fight, but you sure as hell better end it.*

As one of the men drew close and reached out to grab him, Parker bashed him in the head with the gun. The first man stumbled back, as the other one came forward. Just as Parker was about to react to that man, he took a blow to the back of the head.

Molly must have snuck up behind him.

His world spun and he staggered. He saw purple and blue, and then black.

He fell forward onto the wooden floor, drowning into utter darkness.

SEVENTEEN

When Parker came to, a splitting pain erupted in the back of his skull. He felt a pulse, a heartbeat in his temples and his head lay limp. He could not muster the energy to lift his head from hanging forward. He wanted to reach up and massage his temples, but he couldn't. Something was impairing him. Apart from all of his limbs feeling as though they'd been filled with sand, his hands were bound behind his back.

He tried to recall what had happened. With his head spinning, his eyes blinked open. His eyelids were heavy, and with them half closed, he looked down at the floor. It was concrete? *Maybe.*

His vision blurred. But began to make out his surroundings, and the metal chair that both his legs were tied to using rope.

Rope? How old school... He tried to wrestle his arm out again. The binds were tight. There was no way he'd be able to pull out of them.

The floor was definitely concrete, or stone, that of a basement. And when the smell of chemicals subsided from his nostrils, he was able to inhale the musty, watery, smell of the room. *They drugged me?* He thought back to the beginning of his journey when he'd joked about being in a Liam Neeson movie. *Karma...*

He *was* in a basement.

He pulled his head up and looked around. One single hanging light suspended from the ceiling. Straight ahead was a dilapidated set of wooden stairs that led up to two slates of wood on hinges for the door. From the cracks in the wood, it appeared to lead outside.

Just then, he recalled what he couldn't remember before he was knocked unconscious.

Back in the cabin.

The gun.

Blackness.

The door to the cellar swung open. He squinted as beams of sunlight spotlighted all the dust particles in the air. Two sets of legs came down the stairs, and Parker strained to catch sight of who they belonged to.

160

One was a woman. Gray tennis shoes and the ankle skin peeking out was a black complexion.

"Mol—" he started, then retracted his voice as his throat ached from the dryness. He was sore all over.

"We didn't want it to have to be this way," she said softly. She approached him.

He lifted his head to look at her. "I knew... I knew you were one of them now. When we met in Kansas City..."

She crouched to be at his face-level. "All we need to know is where he is, Parker. It doesn't have to be so hard," she coaxed.

He shook his head. "We've been over this. I... don't... know," he said quietly. "Where am I, anyway?"

"We're in Oakland."

He tried to recall where Oakland was. Across the bay from San Francisco. Former home to the Oakland Raiders football team. Rivals to the Chiefs.

"I hate Oakland," he said under his breath.

She smirked. "Well good. Because we aren't staying here for long." Her voice was smooth and confident.

He didn't trust it. He didn't believe that she could so easily turn on Greysen, somebody she loved, or so he had claimed they loved each other, like this.

Edrick must have had some sort of leverage on her. "What?" he painfully let out.

The other man that had come with her stood at the bottom of the stairs. Parker couldn't get a good look at him because he was in the shadow.

"If you cooperate, it's going to go a lot smoother for you," Molly said. "You haven't done anything wrong, Parker. Yet." She lowered her voice. "I just need you to tell me what information you have about his whereabouts. Please. I don't want them to hurt you."

He looked into her eyes so close to his face. There was no way out of this. He didn't want to betray Greysen after everything they'd been through, but part of him was angry with the man. If he'd just come out and faced the men who were after him long ago, they wouldn't have been interested in Parker at all.

"Give it a rest, Molly," the man at the door said, his voice gruff as if he was a smoker. "We'll find out soon enough."

Parker watched her breath and saw her neck and jaw clench when the man behind her said that.

She looked back at Parker with a glint of fear in her eye. "Yeah..." she said quietly. "I'm sorry it has to be this way—"

"It *doesn't* have to be this way," Parker pleaded, his voice shaking. He didn't dare blink.

She looked away from his gaze. "I'm sorry," she mouthed. She stood up and turned from his chair.

"Molly!" Parker yelled out. His heart raced.

She ignored him. She started up the stairs, the man following closely behind.

The hanging door slammed behind them, leaving him in the dim light of the basement once more.

As he sat with his head hanging, a drip of water repeatedly sounded behind him. The dripping of some pipe into a puddle underneath made a distinct pattern in Parker's head, over and over and over again.

It was making him crazy.

We aren't staying here for long...

He replayed Molly's words. What did that mean? If he was taken somewhere else, it was all over. There was no way for him to contact anybody. His parents would never know what had happened to him. Noriana would never know. Greysen, even. His only hope was that

Jack would report him missing when he arrived at the cabin to find Parker gone. The place would be a mess, ransacked. Surely Jack would suspect foul play. Though he wouldn't have any clue as to where Parker might have been taken.

Parker, himself, didn't know where he was being taken. All of his thoughts were foggy with the effects of being hit in the head, and the chemicals they'd used to knock him out, still clouding up his brain.

It wasn't long before they came back for him. He was so tired, hungry, and weak that when the men cut the ropes binding his wrists and ankles, he slinked off the chair and collapsed onto the ground.

He remembered little of the trunk of the car and the sound of airplanes taking off from a runway. He didn't even fight when he was carried up the stairs onto the private jet and dropped in the back with a man who smelled of whisky. Everything was clouded in his mind, but he couldn't fight. He didn't even try.

And he knew, once they cleared the runway, took off in the air, with the pain in his eardrums from the pressure popping in his brain, that it was the end for him. Wherever they were taking him, nobody would ever find his body.

EIGHTEEN

When he woke up again, smell was the first sense he regained. He smelled sterility. His eyes blinked open, and he looked around at the white walls. There was a machinery station next to him, with a curtain that blocked his view from the rest of the room.

A hospital.

I've been rescued! He was overcome with emotion and happiness as he stretched his posture in the bed to attempt to see around the curtain. Only the sharp soreness in his shoulders and ribs caught him off-guard, bringing him back to reality.

There was a mirror off to his left-hand side. He caught a glimpse of himself. He looked rough. Black and blue, bruised eye and a fat lip, with a white gauze bandage wrapped around his head in multiple layers.

A feeling of insecurity overwhelmed him when he realized both arms were strapped down in restraints, and his legs, too.

A woman wearing a white lab coat came around the curtain and adjusted his head bandage.

"Wha—" he began, moaning.

"Whoa, you need to take it easy. I would suggest that you stay quiet." The woman was thin with long blonde hair. Her cheekbones were high and her lips thin. She was older than he'd thought she was at first glance.

She continued, "Somebody will be in shortly to talk to you. You need to rest for now." She walked over to the other side of the bed and moved the sheet down.

He realized he wore a hospital gown now. He didn't even remember being changed. It made him uneasy. He had a killer headache behind his eyes and it hurt to keep them open, yet he didn't dare take his eyes off the nurse. He watched her twist his arm in the restraint for his forearm to face the ceiling. She slapped the inside crease of his arm where it bent at his elbow, trying to inflame his veins. She turned to a medical tray and grabbed a tourniquet. She tied it above his elbow and pulled tight. Then she reached into her pocket and pulled out the needle.

166

Parker flinched. If there was anything he hated, it was needles.

She patted his chest and shushed him.

He couldn't move anyway because of his restraints.

He hated her.

He hated her face.

He hated her high cheek bones and thin lips.

Her straggly blond hair and her nurse hands.

She took the needle and lay the cold tip of it on his arm.

He pinched his eyes closed as the burning, painful sensation in his arm signaled she had pierced the needle through his skin and into his vein. He opened his eyes again to see her taping it off, the needle keeping a continuous hole in his vein, hooked up to a tube that led to a computer.

Parker frowned, the fear turning liquid in his belly. *Wait, why do I need an IV?*

He watched the nurse crinkle up the paper from the bandage and throw it on the tray near the computer stand.

She looked up at him without a single flinch of her features, and then turned and swooshed the curtain closed behind her.

Parker lay in the hospital bed, confused and beyond vulnerable. Was he saved? Why wouldn't the nurse talk to him? She'd told him somebody would be in to talk to him soon.

As if just thinking about it made it come true, a man walked into the room and through the curtain. He was tan, with black hair and a thick black beard. His eyes were intense, and his shoulders were broad. When he spoke with just a slight hint of a Hispanic accent, nobody needed to tell Parker who it was.

"So sorry we have to meet during these circumstances," the man said quietly, walking up to the computer screen and typing in a passcode.

"You're Edrick Crowder," Parker croaked.

The man turned and smiled at him, the crow's feet by his eyes creasing deeply. "I read your book. There were some falsities in it," he said coldly.

"Everything was false. It was a freakin' fiction novel," Parker snapped back.

It was clear by now that he was not safe here, after all. He'd been taken to some sort of facility were Edrick and whatever was left of his crew were hiding out and rebuilding. Just how much they'd rebuilt was still a mystery.

The restraints holding Parker into this bed became even more ominous than before.

"Now you and I both know that sentence in itself is fiction," Edrick said. "It's time to cut the shit, Parker."

Parker craned his neck to try and see the computer screen. "Okay, you wanna hear the whole story? Fine. I'll tell you the *whole* story."

Edrick stopped typing on the computer and looked over at him, raising his eyebrow.

"I met Greysen one time. That's the goddamn truth. He gave me a lot of money to write that book. Then I never saw him again. He lives off the grid. And I can clearly see why he would do that now. I don't have access to where he is. He's like a ghost. He comes and goes. If he wants to be found, he will show himself. I don't think you, or I, or Molly, will ever be able to find him again."

Edrick smiled again. It was not the comforting kind. "That's a cute story. But this guy will let me know if it's true or not." He tapped the side of the computer monitor.

Shit. That must be the invention Greysen was telling me about. He felt a muscle in his lower back spasming. He didn't even know what had happened to his body over the last few days. In fact, he'd lost track of the days all together. Had

Jack gone back to the cabin yet and discovered him gone?

That was his only hope, that Jack had seen the cabin in the state it was in, then contacted Noriana, who would then find Greysen, who would then come to his rescue. Man, that was a long shot.

"Greysen Price was one of the best thinkers I had working for me. It's a shame how he screwed me over. He could have been a rich man."

Parker balled his hands into fists and yanked at the restraints. "You're still just missing the point. Greysen didn't give two shits about the money. He cared about helping people."

Edrick laughed. "Well he certainly helped a lot of people." His sarcasm was killing. "Just like how he helped you by giving you all that money. Now look where we are."

"No, this has nothing to do with him," Parker mumbled. "I always seem to get myself in the wrong places at the wrong times." *Wow. Voicing it out loud really brings perspective.*

"Let's get down to business now," Edrick said in monotone, slapping the top of the monitor.

Parker saw Edrick checking different parts of the set-up. The man looked from the monitor up to the bag that held the IV. He tugged lightly on the cord that connected to Parker's arm.

Parker flinched as Edrick moved the needle in his arm. He didn't know what to do. He was strapped in. *Stall him...* "So what happened to your company after Greysen destroyed the motherboard, anyway?" he asked.

Edrick paused in his preparations. His eyes were stone cold as they locked on Parker. "He caused quite a mess for us, but it didn't stop our operations. He was stupid enough not to think we had a backup. You see, there of course was the physical brain of our operations, which was at my residence that Greysen ruined, but we had a lot backed up in cloud computing, too. And a lot of that was blueprints of future inventions that hadn't gotten exercised just yet. Like this one here." He nodded toward the computer. Then, he checked both sides of the bed restraints as he stood to Parker's side. "See, scientists did a study on rats. They discovered that memories, particularly phobias, could be passed on through generations through our genomes. They found this out by shocking the rats every time they smelled a cherry blossom tree." His sharp nails came down on Parker's leg as he got excited at the word 'shocking'.

Parker flinched yet again.

"Then they bred the rats. After separating the offspring from the parents, they discovered the babies had just as big of a fear of the cherry blossoms, even though they'd never had any experience with them before."

As his story went on, Parker became more and more tense. He didn't need it spelled out to him to know what was going to happen to him. And there was nobody here to save him.

Edrick went around the machine and grabbed a head device, a shower cap looking hat with suctions and wires protruding from it. He rounded the hospital bed and grabbed Parker's neck.

Parker tried to move back and forth to break the man's grip, but Edrick picked up his head and slammed it on the bed.

Parker squeezed his eyes shut. "I didn't do anything to you!" he yelled out, as Edrick began strapping the contraption onto his skull. Two cold, metal suctions sat at his temples. The straps were tight under his chin. "This is barbaric! I'm not a rat!"

"I can see that." Edrick came around the bed and smiled. "Hence the use of this machine. You don't need to *rat* out your friend; we'll just extract the memories from you. The problem is—we haven't technically had time to do many tests on it. Quite frankly, our only human test subject so far has been Molly."

A chill slinked up Parker's spine. *Molly?*

"Did you really think she would give away information about her precious lover? No. We had to pry it from her brain. We found out about their sweet little rendezvous in Paris, and the flowers, so we played on that and put out roses to see if Greysen had been lurking around that city."

Parker bit the inside of his cheek to stop from yelling out. He recalled that Greysen had known it wasn't really Molly. They had used her memories against him just like he'd thought.

"But, because we haven't tested too many subjects out, we aren't quite sure of the consequences. First of all, we can't determine how to sort through memories, so we just take everything. Secondly, we aren't quite sure as to whether or not you keep the memories once we extract them."

Parker jerked against the restraints again.

Edrick grinned and turned to the computer.

"Why would you do this!?" Parker yelled out, not even entirely sure anything he said mattered from this point. "You just want to find Greysen so you can kill him? Is that what this is about? Revenge? What do you gain here?" It was stupid to try and reason with Edrick, but Parker couldn't help trying. It was like the man had blinders on to the rest of the world. He only wanted what he wanted and he had such a one-track mind. Tunnel vision into the one and only goal he had.

"I think you're bluffing," Parker said then at Edrick's continued silence. "I think it's just you and the two other macho guys back there running this whole operation. You want me to believe that you've got your entire business up and running again?"

Edrick stopped clicking his fingers on the keyboard and turned to Parker once more. "I don't need to prove to you my logic, Parker. You are just merely a game piece in the big picture. We're calling the invention Paying the Price. Get it? Paying the Price, Greysen Price?"

"Yeah, Prick," Parker spat. "I get it. It's easy to terrorize your victims when you drug them every time you want to change locations." An annoying pulse ached at the back of his skull.

Edrick typed into the computer, then turned and checked the IV tube that was hooked into Parker's arm once more. He followed the yellowing liquid from the box at the top, down the tube, and into Parker's bloodstream.

174

Parker's heart pounded fiercely in his chest, but only for a moment before he seemed to be suddenly taken from the room.

NINETEEN

Everything was cloudy. He was still present in the hospital room, though everything was blurry as he lay in a sickly, drunk-feeling stupor. His brain couldn't function, and it was as though he was underwater, pawing his way up to the surface, only for it to rise further and further away from his reach.

Time sped up, then slowed down. He had no idea what time it was, or what day, or how long he'd been dazed and running circles in his own mind.

Brain patterns scrawled across a piece of paper as it printed from the machine to his left, tracing every emotion he felt as it racked his brain for memories, experiences, and phobias. And though every one of his senses was impaired beyond his control, he still felt an underlining anger. His privacy was being violated. All his thoughts and emotions that belonged to him and only him were being taken and viewed against his will. He tried to fight it, and was successful in at least keeping it stagnant for a while, but then the drunken feeling seeped further and further into his veins, pulling and tugging at his memories.

Though horrifying and ultimately traumatizing, Parker still had his own soul in there. The whole of his being remained intact, regardless the excavation of his history. *That means... that Molly is still in there somewhere as well.* And despite it all, he couldn't help but be curious in how the machine worked.

It was as though you could take a whole group of people and put them in a room. All of their experiences—life story, fears, hopes, and dreams, were all collected into a book for each person. Some people's lives were horror stories. Some were romances. Some were thrillers, and some were instruction manuals.

There was a quote about writing Parker had heard once that had stuck with him, and that occurred to him now:

"There's nothing to writing. All you have to do is sit at a typewriter and open a vein."

And this invention used to harness memories and experience was exactly that.

Parker was exhausted and drained, as though just lying there was so much work. He heard muffled voices at the end of the tunnel, then they began to get louder and clearer. He pried his eyes open. *Where am I...?*

He looked over and saw nothing but red covering his arm and the sheets beneath. Somebody had ripped the IV needle from his arm. Just as he was about to pull at his restraints, Molly threw herself over him.

Parker inhaled, afraid of her at first, then realizing she was unhooking his restraints.

"We don't have much time," she whispered. As she leaned over him, he noticed a deep purple bruise under her eye on her cheekbone. She'd been hit pretty hard.

She undid the restraints on both of his arms and then moved on to his legs.

He slowly sat up; his head pounded and felt as though he'd just been weighed down by a ton of bricks. He looked around the room and saw Edrick face-first on the floor, a pool of blood coming out from underneath his head. "Is he...?" Parker whispered.

She shook her head. "I—I don't know. I couldn't—I had to," she stammered.

Parker noticed for the first time that she was

really shaking. "Hey, it's gonna be okay," he slurred, still groggy.

"We have to go!" she yelled with urgency, then grabbed his hand and tugged.

"Molly, I don't know if I can walk—" He tried to move his legs over the edge of the bed. "I'm numb all over."

"Just—you have to try! You're too heavy for me to carry," she urged him through gritted teeth.

He hit his legs with his hands to try and bring back sensation in them. It'd been too soon since he'd been drugged to try and walk. Though he really had no choice if he wanted to get out of there alive.

Apart from his sense of privacy being violated, he really didn't give a shit if Edrick watched his memories. The man would find Greysen sooner or later, anyway.

What most worried Parker was the fact that once they'd gotten everything they needed out of him, he'd be in a position where he knew too much, more so than he already did. And what did bad guys normally do with people who knew too much and had no other purpose? *Kill them.*

Or turn them into puppets like they'd done with Molly. Parker wasn't interested in either of those two options.

He wanted to get back to Noriana.

And his writing.

And his awkward, average life.

He was able to stand at last, using the bed to stabilize himself. A tingling sensation surged throughout his body, the same feeling he'd get when he'd cross his legs for too long and it cuts off circulation. It tickled and tingled. He didn't like it.

Molly came up under him and allowed him to use her as a crutch.

He put his arm around her neck and hopped off the bed. "Okay, I think I can do this..." He let go of her and took baby steps. "If anything, I can crawl," he whispered over to her.

"Hang on, let me get my crowbar back," she said, looking over at Edrick face-down on the floor. The large metal bar was next to him.

Parker crouched down to stabilize himself. Just as he made way for a side door that was already cracked open, somebody came through the other door across the room. He froze dead in his tracks.

"What the hell is going on here?" The man towered in the doorway. He was a muscle cliché, no doubt Edrick's replacement of Dolor after Dolor had perished in that parking garage a year back. He was bald-headed, broad-shouldered, and thin-waisted, and his muscles strained the seams of his shirt.

Parker looked in a panic over at Molly, who picked up the crowbar.

"Peyton, go—go get help!" she yelled.

Huh? Parker looked back and forth from Molly to the giant man in the doorway, who must have been Peyton.

"This monster—" she pointed over to Parker with the crowbar, and he gaped at her in shock, "I came back to check on Edrick as he harnessed the boy's memories and I found him attacking Edrick! He got to him before I could help."

The man tilted his head as if contemplating whether or not he believed her.

Molly walked back over to Parker and grabbed a chunk of his shirt in her fist.

He fell to his knees at her side. One, he hadn't been expecting it. Two, he was already unstable. His head was still pounding. At least they'd had the courtesy of bandaging it up from the previous knock-out before moving on.

Parker kept his crossed eyes focused on the floor tiles as Molly held him by the back of his shirt. Something moved in his peripheral vision. He strained to look over at the side door he'd tried to escape out before. For a moment, he thought he'd been hallucinating. He wanted to get out of there so badly that he was dreaming up a rescue.

It wasn't until Greysen dove out from behind the door and tackled Molly to the floor that he believed the man was really there.

It happened so fast that the muscle man in the doorway didn't even have time to react.

Parker watched in disbelief as Greysen sat on Molly's stomach. She didn't say a word, even if she could.

They stared into each other's eyes with such longing and intensity as Greysen dug his fingers into her neck, directly on her pulse. It wasn't long before her eyes rolled into the back of her head and she went limp.

Parker was speechless and couldn't believe his eyes. *What is happening!? Molly isn't bad! She was saving me!* But then, he didn't understand why she'd ratted him out to Peyton and lied about what had happened to Edrick. Was Molly good? Was she bad?

Parker ducked behind the hospital bed as the muscle man finally sprang into action, launching himself across the room toward Greysen.

Molly's head rolled to the side as Peyton's fat arm came down behind Greysen.

He jumped off Molly onto the floor, then used

his legs to kick off Peyton's stomach. The big muscled man let out an *"oomph*!" as Greysen pushed himself up to standing.

The man was thin. Parker had only ever seen him wearing large, oversized winter coats or baggy clothing. He had thinned out in the ribs, and still sported a long beard.

Peyton faced Greysen now, and looked as if he'd seen a ghost.

Was *Parker* seeing a ghost? He was definitely in another one of those wrong-place-at-the-wrong-time situations that had so often been happening in his everyday life now-a-days. And once again, he felt like he was a character in an action flick.

He watched Greysen and Peyton struggle on the ground, throwing punches at each other. Peyton was heavier and clumsier than Greysen, who could move about with ease and stealth. Regardless, Peyton eventually wrestled Greysen to the ground and pinned him, his hands around his neck to choke him, while also repeatedly slamming his head into the ground.

Shit, he's losing! Parker snapped out of his trance behind the bed. *I have to do something!* He sprang into action. Without being noticed, he crawled over to Molly, who he realized was still breathing, just passed out, and grabbed the crowbar. The other two men were too busy trying to kill each other to notice Parker moving close to the ground.

Just as he saw the blood rush away from Greysen's face, his legs kicking from underneath Peyton, Parker pulled the crowbar back and whacked the muscle man hard on the skull with it. A splatter of blood hit the wall behind him as his head jerked forward, and then he slumped over onto Greysen, going still.

Greysen took that opportunity to shove Peyton off him.

What did I just do? Parker began to shake uncontrollably. He dropped the crowbar with a loud clang and looked down at his hands as they trembled.

Greysen regained his breath, choking out the air. "Hey! You're—look at me Parker."

Parker looked into the man's gray eyes, breaths coming in heaves.

"You're okay. You're going to be okay."

Parker nodded his head up and down in recognition, though he certainly didn't feel like he was going to be okay at the moment. "What did you...?" He looked over at Molly.

Greysen followed his gaze with painful admiration. "She's okay, too. I understand pressure points. I just put her to sleep. She's alive.

I did it for her protection."

Just as he said that, a moan rang out from the other side of the room.

It was Edrick. He began to stir.

"Shit! Help me, Parker!" Greysen yelled, hurrying over to Edrick's body.

"That's not my fight to finish!" Parker said shakily.

"I'm not going to kill him... just yet. Hurry!"

Parker was sick of everyone telling him he needed to hurry. "What then? What do I do?"

Greysen motioned to Edrick. "Help me get him up on the bed."

He hesitated a moment before he scrambled to help.

Together, they dragged the man off the floor and up onto the bed. Greysen grabbed the restraints and strapped down Edrick's flopping arms and limp legs. Then he grabbed the headgear piece and placed it over his boss's head.

"Are you going to kill him?" Parker whispered, looking from Greysen to the door and back again as if anyone could come in at any minute.

Greysen turned to the computer. "I've killed enough people in my lifetime. The only time I feel like it's right is if my life or that of someone I love is in immediate danger." It sounded as if he was daydreaming as he spoke.

Parker kept a watchful eye on the position of the crowbar to the position of the door. "How did you find me here?"

"We can talk about that later." Greysen fumbled with the computer. "This... this is amazing," he said slowly. "There are many inventions I've created, but to actually see the product off the paper, out of my mind, and working functionally in front of me..." He shook his head in awe. "Of course, there are a few adjustments I'd change in the design... most obviously the restraints. This machine was supposed to be for people who requested it. They would *want* to harness their many years of knowledge and memories to pass down to their loved ones. This invention was in no way, shape, or form meant to be used to invade people's privacy and take away memories that belonged to only them. There were many flaws in this, hence the reason I didn't think the world was ready for it." Greysen looked back at the computer and then at Edrick. "How do I even do this?" he asked, looking up at Parker.

"You came up with this invention!" Parker rocked back on his heels and put his hand out on the frame of the bed to stabilize himself. He side glanced over at Peyton's body, a sickening feeling clouding his stomach.

"Yeah, but I never actually put together the admin. You just went through it, right?"

"It's an IV. You have to put in an IV and then some kind of drug that makes you feel drunk. It makes you feel like you're dreaming. I didn't like the smell of the chemicals, though. And your entire body feels like bags of sand are in it." He walked over and picked up the tube that had been previously in his arm. The bloody needle was on the end of it—the one that had been ripped out of his arm.

He looked down at his arm now, remembering the recent pain as he saw the dried blood stains. He'd never had a moment to bandage it up. The crease in his arm had already begun to turn into a deep purple bruise. The so-called "nurse" hadn't been careful with him.

"Shit..." Greysen breathed, grabbing the tube from him. "I'm not good with needles."

"What do you want to see in his head?" Parker asked hesitantly.

Greysen paused, then looked at him in the eyes. "I destroyed what I thought was his entire company years ago. Little did I know the hell my life was to become after leaving that mansion. Leaving *him* alive. I thought that destroying all his computers would stop him, but now I know. Therefore, I want to see what else I need to destroy to keep him from hurting any more people."

Just like the technology servers that control all of our lives today, Parker thought. *We've become so dependent on technology, and just when we think we've deleted something that may come back to haunt us, we realize you can never really delete it.* He related with this sentiment on a *hardcore* level. He was without a phone since he'd chucked it in the toilet. And he'd felt the urge to grab the phantom phone out of his pocket at every turn he made. "We should get out of here. Somebody's going to come if we don't, and what about Molly?!"

"I'll deal with Molly later," Greysen said coldly.

"She was helping me escape though..." He walked around the bed and joined Greysen at the computer. "She was only pretending when that other guy came back—"

"You don't need to explain it to me," Greysen snapped over his shoulder at him. He was mad about something, that much was clear. Though when he'd choked Molly out, she hadn't fought him. She'd allowed him to do it. Either she trusted him to take care of her, or she truly felt like she deserved whatever was going to happen to her.

After an awkward moment of silence, Parker realized Greysen was fumbling with the tube. "Hey," he said, "there was a nurse that did mine, want me to go see if I can find her?"

Greysen stared at him in thought as Edrick stirred, moaning from his head wound. "She'd recognize you, no? Maybe I should do it. I'm less recognizable."

Parker scoffed. "I mean... everyone knows you here. Hell, that Peyton guy looked as though he'd seen a ghost when he saw you! But I guess it's worth a shot." He nodded. "I can stay in here with these three." He looked down at all the unconscious people in the room.

Molly on the ground looking as if she were asleep, Peyton bleeding, and Edrick strapped to the bed in pain.

Greysen dropped the tube and walked towards the adjacent door he'd come through before.

"How will you know where to look?" Parker asked.

"Because I've worked in this building for over ten years," he said quietly.

It hit Parker then.

He knew he'd been brought to Chicago after he'd been drugged back in Oakland, but he'd had no clue where. It just struck him that he was inside Humavision. The very place where the book he'd written about Greysen had taken place. They must have remodeled some of the rooms into looking like hospital wards. The thought sent a chill up his spine. *What else happened in this building?*

And it must have been such a risk, and so hard for Greysen to return here. However, he did have the advantage of knowing this building like the back of his hand, even if things had been remodeled.

Right before he left the room, Greysen turned to him, "Hey. You know how to use one of these?" He threw a small handheld gun at him.

"Geesh!" He cupped it to his chest to catch it, then pulled it back to look at it. "Use a gun? Yeah, I know how to use one," he lied. Why did people keep handing him guns? If anything, he could use it to hit somebody with. Maybe knock somebody out. There seemed to be a lot of that going around these days.

And with that, Greysen was gone.

TWENTY

Parker listened to the soft hum of the machine on the side of the bed, as Edrick pulled at the restraints.

He wasn't fully conscious yet, but every time he made a noise, Parker leapt out of his skin. He held the gun by his side and looked every which way, worried that somebody besides Greysen or the nurse would come through those doors at any moment. What would he do then? What if he was captured again? If they were in Greysen's old work building, how many people did Edrick still have working for him?

Even though Greysen had destroyed the mother board at Edrick's mansion, which must have been a huge chore for him, Edrick must have gone to work the next day as if nothing had happened.

He had a lot of money, he knew a lot of powerful people. Parker was almost certain now that Edrick had just continued on as if nothing had happened, and even with the minor setback, had continued business as usual. Nobody at the company had known what had happened that night, except that Greysen was now a convicted child kidnapper on the run, and that they needed to catch him before he went off the map.

Parker wasn't sure why Edrick had put Greysen on the news as a wanted man, except to maybe make it harder for him to hide. But why would he do that when he could have just sent a privately paid hit man to kill him without the eyes of the media on him?

Regardless, in the end, Edrick hadn't found him. He'd had to take other measures in order to get to him. And they'd worked.

Greysen had come out of the wood work. He had shown his face here again.

Parker jostled the mouse for the computer, and just as the screen woke up from its slumber, a screen saver of the Humavision logo bounced around the screen.

Edrick also became more coherent. "My... my head," he whispered with a rasp.

Parker looked back at him. "Yeah, it hurts, doesn't it?" He pointed up to the bandage around his own head. And even though Edrick was still drowsy from the blow, Parker saw his spirit behind his eyes, and he was pissed off.

He pulled at the restraints.

"Getting a taste of your own medicine, asshole," Parker snapped. He looked over the main face of the monitor and saw icon after icon of people's names and dates. They'd used this machine on more people than they'd let on. In fact, he wouldn't have been surprised if Edrick had made every employee administer their memories in efforts to make sure they weren't betraying the company. They'd probably had to sign something they didn't know they were agreeing to, to be able to keep their jobs. Giving up their privacy.

It was easy to find his own file because it was the last one taken. He clicked on it and it brought up a chart of brain patterns and an entire log of the make-up of his brain. He couldn't even fathom what he was looking at, except that it was essentially home-video diaries of his entire life. It was mind blowing, to say the least.

"Boring, if you ask me." Edrick spoke in short spurts.

"Oh, good," he responded, vulnerability creeping its way up his spine and wrapping itself around his neck. "What gives you the right to just steal people's memories and experiences? These aren't yours. You had no right!"

"You had information I wanted," he choked. "I don't even care about you, kid. I just wanted Greysen Price."

It was as if by saying the name, he'd summoned Greysen into the room, because through the door came the blonde nurse from earlier, and she was as white as the lab coat she wore.

Parker's heart sank into his gut and his arm instinctually lifted the gun at her. From out behind her came Greysen, who also had a gun pointed at the back of her neck.

"Oh, didn't realize you had it handled." Parker slowly put his arm down. He turned back to the computer and dragged the file named after him to the trash can on the monitor. For some reason he knew that even if he did this small step, it would never actually be deleted. Information was always out there in some server once it'd been sent once.

There was no avoiding it. The public was given a sense of power when they were able to delete what they wanted: pictures off their phones, text messages, emails; but it was never really deleted.

He noticed the woman was shaking, and lacked all of the confidence about her that she'd had earlier when she was administering his IV. When she saw Edrick in the bed, her eyes welled up and her lip quivered.

"Come on, Allie, let's get this done sooner rather than later," Greysen said lowly, though he wasn't harsh.

Parker knew Greysen hated having leverage on people that had nothing to do with the situation, but he needed her.

"I just need you to hook him up," Greysen said to her.

She looked up at him with disgust.

"Don't you dare do it, Al," Edrick choked. The two stared each other.

They walked over to the computer, and Parker decided to go back the other way, behind them to the door they'd just come through. He stood at the door with the gun, figuring he'd be of more use to them if he played the look out. It was now Greysen's turn to deal with the situation. After all, the reason they were here was because of the mess he was a part of in the first place.

The nurse called Allie looked back and forth from the two. Greysen used force to hold the gun up to her forehead. He was in a deadly mode. A mode Parker had never seen in reality before. He had been one of the most genuine people he'd ever met, and seeing Greysen in this aggressive state startled him. He knew it was necessary, and that he was essentially fighting for the upper hand in his own life, but it was still jarring.

"If you pull any tricks while we're hooking you up, Edrick, I will kill her," he said.

Parker looked over at Allie just then, who was pale and appeared to have her breath held.

"I don't care," Edrick spat.

Allie began to cry. "What the hell, Ed?" she yelled.

Parker's ears perked up. They must have had more of a relationship than strictly professional.

"After everything we've been through?" she screeched. "What, do you just screw whatever girl you want and then toss them to the side?"

Edrick said nothing. The tension in the air was thick, stinging.

Then, without any more coercion, Allie sprang into action, pulling the medical tray to her and putting on the blue powdered gloves.

"Stop that!" Edrick spat.

She looked at him, and then said to Greysen, "I'll help you. Please. Just—"

"Allie, you know I can't trust you," he said evenly. "I have to keep this gun on you. Just in case."

Even though she now seemed to have the confidence she'd had before, she nodded, her eyes welling up again. She sniffled, shaking as she clanked through the medical tools for a needle that was still in plastic. She opened it and moved in on Edrick. She unscrewed Parker's bloody needle and attached the new one. Then, she grabbed his arm and stuck him with the needle. He thrashed about.

"You bitch!" he yelled.

She bent down and picked up the tube that was attached to the machine. After she secured the needle into his arm and wrapped the white gauze around and around so it wouldn't move out of place, she went to his head and grabbed the sides of his face, forcing him to look up at her.

"Allie, I'm sorry," he muttered. "Please. You are my only lover. I was just bluffing, calling Price's bluff, saying I didn't care if you died—"

"Shut up," she said, tears rolling down her cheeks. She strapped his head down. She walked back to the rolling cart the computer was on, then looked at Greysen. "He's ready." She looked back over to the computer screen, her eyes crazy, before she tempered them again and put her head down.

He hit the trigger that released the serum into the IV. The liquid trailed down the tube and into Edrick's bloodstream.

The three of them, Parker, Greysen, and Allie, watched as his body finally went limp, and the lines began to take form on the computer screen. Pretty soon, they would have access to every piece of information needed to destroy this man and his company, if only to save just one more person from his wrath.

TWENTY-ONE

P arker sat on the floor, weak in the knees and legs trembling. He couldn't shake the terrible splitting headache that pulsed at the back of his skull. He closed his eyes while he continued to listen to the beeping of the computer currently still harnessing Edrick's memories.

He was beyond exhausted and would rather be anywhere else besides here.

Greysen walked over and put his hand on his shoulder. "It'll be over soon, and we can go. I need to get you and Molly to a safe place. We need to get you checked out, but it's probably not smart to go to a hospital. A lot of my allies in Chicago have dried up..."

The thought instantly popped into Parker's mind, even before he could offer any solutions. "I know," he said quietly. "Is it safe to make a phone call?"

Greysen nodded to the door that he had entered through. "It's the back hallway you came through. Nobody will even think to come down that way. Just go outside the door and keep your voice down. Don't worry, hang in there and we'll get help soon."

He felt his pant pockets and his heart sank. "My phone. I threw it in a toilet."

Greysen raised his eyebrow but didn't question him. He looked around the room, back at Allie who was watching them. Then he walked over and knelt down by Molly. He turned her limp body and found her phone in her back pocket. He held it in front of her face a moment to unlock the phone using face recognition, then stood up and tossed it to him.

He caught it and made his way out the door, then slowly closed it behind him. He leaned against the wood of the door and slid down to the floor. His legs were still Jell-O.

The phone rang, and when he heard his brother answer on the other line, a lump caught in his throat and his voice cracked. "Stephen?" he asked, hardly able to contain himself. He allowed his tears to fall, and wiped them away as he pushed the phone up to his ear.

"What the hell, Parker? Where are you? Are you okay?"

"I'm... I'm okay. Please don't ask me any questions, I just need to know... if you can help? How long would it take you to get to Chicago?"

The line was quiet a moment. "Are you injured?" Stephen asked.

"I, uhhh, I have a pretty bad crack on the back of my head, it's been really hurting."

"Jesus, Parker. I can be there in three, maybe four hours. If you can't get to a hospital, I can call ahead for you and get you set up with a—"

"I can't, Stephen... I just, can't. You said if I ever needed help with anything, that—"

"Yeah. I'm coming, Bro. Make sure you apply pressure to the back of your head, okay? If you feel light-headed or dizzy, like you're going to pass out, don't give in, okay? Don't allow yourself to lose consciousness. You have somebody with you, at least?"

"Yeah." He reached up and brushed under his nose with the back of his hand.

"Okay, how will I know where to find you?"

"Uh, I'll give you another call in a few hours, okay? I need to figure out where we are going next. We can't stay here."

"Okay. I'll be waiting."

Parker tapped the *end* button. It had been so nice to hear one of his family member's voices.

The realization all at once just sunk in. *I'm okay. I'm alive.*

And even though they most definitely weren't out of the woods just yet, Greysen was here, and for some reason that made him feel better. They had the upper hand.

He should have gone back into the room, but he wanted to do one more thing first.

He dialed the long, eleven-digit number into Molly's international phone and waited while it connected. It rang multiple times. "Come onnnn," he groaned.

The line clicked. "Hello?"

Her voice was the most comforting thing he could have possibly heard in this moment. "Noriana," he sang quietly.

"Oh my goodness, Parker. Are you okay? Where are you?" Her voice became frantic. "I thought something terrible happened to you. I thought I'd never talk to you again."

"I'm not out of the woods just yet, but Greysen is here with me. He found me," he said quickly and quietly. "You have no idea how great it is just to hear your voice, babe." He smiled.

"My dad... my dad told me about the scene in the cabin. There was blood. Are you okay?" she asked, obviously trying to collect herself.

"Yeah, that was my blood alright. But I'm okay. Stephen's going to come help."

"But he's in Kansas City! You need help now!"

"I'm okay, Nori. I wanted to tell you I was alive. I can't talk long, but—" He heard a loud pop from inside the room behind him. It left a high-pitched ringing in his ears.

A gun shot.

"I have to go! I love you!" He dropped the phone on the floor, shattering the screen. He didn't know whether or not he should open the door, or what exactly had happened. What would he find if he opened that door and Greysen had been shot? There would be no chance for him.

But he had to take the risk. What else was he supposed to do? He shoved the door open and fell back into the room.

Greysen was on the ground, sitting on his butt with his knees up and his hands back on the floor, as if he had just braced himself from a fall. Allie stood in front of him, the gun pointed at him. Edrick was sitting up on the bed out of his restraints, the IV was out and he was turned, watching Allie and Greysen. It seemed as though he had come out of his sleep, and Parker could tell he was just resurfacing from the drugs that felt like dream land. He'd just been there himself, not too long ago.

He wished he hadn't reentered the room.

"You!" Allie yelled, pointing the gun over to Parker. "Get over there with him. Now!"

She didn't have to ask him twice. He scurried over next to Greysen and gave him a look like, *What the hell happened while I was gone?*

"Allie, you don't have to—" Greysen started.

"Shut up!" She gritted her teeth. "Give me that gun!"

Parker looked down at his hand, grasping the gun. He'd completely forgotten about it. He side-glanced at Greysen, then dropped it and kicked it over to her. *Stupid!* he scolded himself.

"C'mon, Allie," Greysen tried again, "we used to work together—"

"Oh, now that the tables have turned, you're going to act all buddy-buddy?" She sounded furious.

"Do you even know how to use that thing?"

She fired the gun into the corner of the room.

"Shhhhit!" Parker yelled, covering his ears.

She must have been the one who'd shot before, too. How she'd gotten the gun from Greysen was beyond him. But she certainly knew how to use it.

"Why are you doing this?" Parker asked as he stared at the floor, avoiding her gaze.

She contemplated the question, and as she rocked back and forth anxiously, she tucked her hair behind her ear and then returned her hand to the gun. "It's clear by now that I'm going to be in some of those memories of his you harnessed," she said coldly.

"Don't you have it over there on the computer?" His voice cracked. His sweaty hands trembled by his sides.

"*He* has it." She stabbed the gun in the air at Greysen.

He looked to him.

"Why'd you help me extract this data then?" Greysen asked.

She waved the gun again. "Because he's a Dick!" She stabbed the gun at Edrick before pointing it back at him. "And... and it worked because it got you to let your guard down."

"What could possibly be on here that could ruin you, Allie? Those aren't the parts we're interested in, anyway," he coaxed.

Parker couldn't understand how Greysen stayed so calm. His voice hadn't the slightest inkling of nerves. It must have been the years and years of working under countless pressure.

He knew how to handle his emotions in dire and demanding situations.

Parker could learn a thing or two from this guy. But their lives were in the hands of an unstable ex-coworker. The unpredictability in the room was what he feared the most.

"That's impossible," she said. She lowered the gun slowly, and just when he thought she was going to set it down, she handed it over to Edrick.

He took the gun with ease and looked up at them.

Parker saw fire in the man's eyes and he grabbed Greysen's arm, sure he was about to die.

It all happened so fast.

In an instant, Edrick scanned the gun over Parker and Greysen, and then moved it to Allie.

"I'm sorry," she cried quietly, putting her hands over her mouth.

The gun fired.

The shot ripped through Allie's chest, sending her backwards. She hit the wall and slid down to the ground, leaving a smearing trail of blood. She heaved in air for a few painful moments, and then let go.

Parker held his breath. He was for sure, next.

Edrick turned the gun around, placed it in his own mouth, and pulled the trigger.

TWENTY-TWO

"**P**arker."

His name was called in the distance. Far away. Down at the end of the tunnel.

"Parker, look at me."

His ears rang, and he reached up and wiped blood from his cheek. He looked down at his hand. It wasn't his blood. It wasn't his blood on his hand. His stomach grew queasy. He looked up into the eyes of Greysen Price, who knelt down at his eye level, a concerned look on his face.

"You have to help me get Molly."

Parker knew he said words, but his ears were ringing and he could only read his lips. His head was hollow, and his insides, a gong that had been struck hard.

"Molly is still alive," Greysen was saying. "And we need to get out of here." He stood up and approached his lover. His ex-lover? He scooped her up and turned to look at Parker, his eyes desperate. He'd just watched his ex-boss die.

"Yeah," Parker croaked, trying with great effort to rouse himself. "Just—just tell me what to do, okay?"

With that, they got straight to work.

Parker slumped in the folding chair and looked out the window at the blinking neon Super 8 motel sign. "How did you know Molly wasn't bad? I thought when you were choking her... you were killing her. I didn't know what to think." He looked over at Molly laying in the motel bed, her back to them. He looked over at Greysen across the small table pick up his Styrofoam cup of coffee and bring it to his lips. He looked down at his own steaming cup. He couldn't fathom swallowing it with this constant lump in his throat.

Greysen sighed and shook his head. "It didn't take long for me to figure out Molly wasn't the one who'd left those roses back in Paris. I knew they had some form of leverage on Molly, whether she straight up told them or they used measures to pry it from her. I didn't know the extent of their progress with the memory machine until I came upon that room." He placed his cup of coffee on the table and leaned toward Parker across the table, his voice low. "And I knew she'd had to gain their trust somehow in order to get access to the inside of Edrick's operations."

He looked down to the table and wet his lips. "I compressed her carotid arteries to make her pass out, is all." He looked over to her, then back to Parker. "I knew the limits, knew I wasn't going to kill her, just knock her out. It was for her own safety. I needed to make it look like she wasn't betraying them, even if it meant hurting her. Because it could have been what saved her life in that instant."

"I don't even want to know how you learned that," Parker said quietly. His body and mind were numb. He traced a scratch on the table with his finger. "How do I go on living with that scene in my head for the rest of my life? I mean Edrick... he..."

He sighed again. He put his hand across the table and laid it over Parker's. "I am... Parker, I am so sorry I brought you into this mess."

It was the first time he had ever heard a crack in Greysen's voice. His sentiment was genuine. "I don't know how you can get that scene out of your mind," he continued gently. "I don't. But I do know that by being here today, you have been a vital part to doing so much good for this world.

The world is a better place with that man gone. I can attest to that first-hand. I know you don't feel the same things I do, and that scene was absolutely horrible, but selfishly... I'm glad I wasn't the one who had to do it."

Parker looked up at him and saw tears in his eyes.

"I'm not a murderer, Parker," he whispered. His bottom lip trembled.

"I know that—"

"I didn't want to be there or see that just as much as you. And I just want to thank you. You will forever be like a son to me."

Parker shook his head. "You don't have to say that."

"No, I'm serious. None of this would have ended for me had I never met you."

He wallowed in his thoughts, moving his gaze from the table, back outside. He watched the cars on the road, hoping one of them would turn into the motel's lot. Hoping the person behind the wheel was Stephen. He just wanted his brother here. Any kind of reminder of home.

When he didn't say anything, Greysen continued, "Ever since that night in the basement of his mansion, my life changed. Not because I escaped, but because it didn't end right there. Sure, I escaped that house, but I was running for my life. And I lived years and years with the guilt of what had happened in the past, working for that man."

"It wasn't your fault, Greysen."

"But it was! I was there. They were *my* ideas."

Parker shifted on his chair. "Well… you are free now." He gave in to the white, Styrofoam cup staring at him. He lifted it to his lips and took a small sip. *Muddy water.* He refrained from making a face and swallowed. It did feel good to have something warm coat his throat.

Greysen nodded, then looked over to Molly, still out cold.

"What do you think happened to her after you left for Paris?" he whispered.

"Maybe she'll tell me. Maybe she won't," he said, matching Parker's voice level. "I can't even fathom, though. I don't even know if we can salvage what feelings we had for each other before all of this."

"Only time will tell," he said.

Greysen nodded again.

Just then, somebody rapped on the door of the motel room, and both men leaped out of their skin.

Parker stood up and went to look out the peephole. He opened the door to his brother Stephen standing in the doorway, emergency

215

medical kit in hand. He threw his arms around him, something that was so unexpected, and without saying a word, Stephen hugged him back.

Stephen then pushed him back a few steps and grabbed him by the chin. As if it were a natural movement of his, he retrieved a flashlight pen from his pocket with his other hand and held it up to Parker's eyes, shining a bright light into each pupil.

He pulled back from his brother's grip and invited him into the room. "I'm alright, Stephen. Just—can you look at Molly first?" He waved a hand toward the unconscious woman, still sprawled on the bed.

Again, Stephen was silent as he crossed the threshold.

He closed the door behind him.

Stephen approached the bedside. As he reached it, Molly turned her head and groaned, her eyes fluttering open.

He knelt to her level and searched her eyes with a look of concern. "Hi there. My name's Doctor Rubec. I'm here to help."

Molly's eyes darted around the room. She tried to push up and fell back down when her gaze landed on Greysen, reaching her hand up to her head.

216

"Easy—" Stephen said calmly as he stood.

Greysen moved in, when Stephen put his hand to Greysen's chest and pushed him back, his brow furrowed.

Parker advanced forward. "He's cool, Stephen."

Stephen looked from Greysen, to Parker, then back. "I don't know you. She's obviously startled. Back-up. Let me do my work."

Greysen looked to Parker and he motioned him back with a nod of his head.

Stephen asked Molly some basic questions about if she knew where she was, her name, what year it was. She seemed to be good in answering all his questions, so he took her vitals, instructed her to rest, and then stood up.

He looked at Greysen and then turned and told his brother, "She's going to be alright. What happened here? Who did this to you guys?"

"It's a long story..." he answered quietly.

Stephen took a good, long look at Parker, and shook his head. "It better be! I dropped everything to hop on a plane and get here, thoughts racing in my mind about what could have possibly happened to my brother! I never thought you'd actually take my offer seriously."

"I needed help." Parker stuffed his hands in his pockets.

217

"Clearly!" He paused then and closed his eyes, taking a deep, slow breath. Then he exhaled and opened his eyes again. "Sorry. I was just... I was really worried, Parker. Come on, you can tell me the whole story while I take a look at what's under your bandage?"

Parker nodded and started to walk towards the bathroom. "Let's give them some privacy," he whispered to Stephen, nodding to Molly and Greysen.

TWENTY-THREE

Greysen

Faster than Parker and his brother could get to the bathroom and close the door, Greysen was at Molly's bedside. He wasn't sure how she would feel about him being there, but he reached for her hand, anyway.

He inhaled sharply when she grabbed it, squeezing it tight. It was enough to send him over the edge, and he allowed his emotion to pour out of him. Everything he'd been holding inside flowed from his eyes and down his cheeks. He laid his forehead down on the bed at her side.

She ran her other hand over his hair.

After he collected himself, he wiped his face on the sheets of the bed and looked up at her, his lip quivering. "I thought you were dead," he said quietly.

"I thought I was too, that day," she said, her voice shaking. She touched his graying beard.

"You don't have to tell me about it... I'm here now. We're together now." He looked hopefully at her and pushed a piece of her hair off her forehead. "I'm sorry I left you. I never would have if I'd known there was hope—"

She cut him off. "I know. Greysen, you don't have to do this."

"I feel like I have to! You have been the only thing on my mind."

"I've done horrible things."

"It wasn't your fault!"

"Greysen. What happened back there? In that room, after you..." She cleared her throat. "How did we get out?"

He looked down. He wasn't sure he wanted to revisit that Humavision room so soon. But he owed it to her. "I let my guard down for only a moment and Allie got the gun from me. Everything was such a blur and it happened so fast." He took a moment to catch his breath. He felt her hanging on to his every word. "Allie gave Edrick the gun. He shot her. Then he turned the gun on himself and blew off his own head." Red. All he could see was red in his mind as he said it. He would never stop seeing that image, as long as he lived.

It sickened him that a kid like Parker had had to see that, too.

"Geeze..." she breathed.

With his head hanging down, he saw her chest rising and falling. Her heart rate had quickened.

"Do you have that chip?" she asked, her voice becoming stronger.

He looked at her, then reached into his pocket and retrieved the chip that had all of Edrick's brain patterns on it. All of his memories.

Emotion overcame Molly. She burst into full-fledged tears, then grabbed at his arm. The one that held the chip.

It took him by surprise, and he tucked the chip back in his pocket and pushed away from the bed. He hadn't realized she'd get so worked up over seeing that he had it in his possession.

"Please. Please don't watch it. Please," she begged.

"My Moll... I— " His voice cracked once more. He paused and drew in a deep breath, then let it out slowly. "Right now is a new beginning."

She turned her head away from him.

"No, listen! I don't care what you've done. It doesn't matter if you've been working for Edrick. I don't care what is on that chip, Molly. We can start over. Right here and right now." He laid his head back down on her ribs.

"I just don't know... I don't know if I can be in a relationship right now. All of this is too much to process," she said quietly, sniffling.

"I understand. Take your time. I don't even know where I go from here. I don't even know where I belong in society now," he said, mostly speaking to himself, but voicing it out loud for the first time. "We can... take it slow," he finished.

They heard a noise come from the bathroom.

Molly glanced that way. "Where did you find the kid and why did you bring him into all of this?"

He actually stifled a laugh. "He was in the wrong place at the wrong time. I overheard him telling some stranger his life story when he was in Paris. I needed help getting my story out there. He was a writer. He was American. And he also... well nevermind. I pursued him. I didn't know what else to do. I had no idea that plan would even go anywhere."

"You really want me to believe that?"

He lifted his head and frowned at her. "What do you mean?"

She sighed. "Stop dragging him along and tell him the damn truth, Greysen."

The truth. What did Molly know about him and his past, before he'd met her? Before he'd even married his ex-wife?

"He's a good guy," she said, looking over to the bathroom door.

"I know," Greysen confirmed. "I owe him my life."

TWENTY-FOUR

P arker sat on the closed toilet lid.
      Stephen set his kit on the sink and
      opened it. He unwrapped the white
gauze bandage around Parker's head.

He winced and sunk his head down, the headache erupting again at the back.

"Hey, can you keep your head up? I know it hurts. Just look at the wall, man." Stephen unwrapped the layers. The gauze was stained with blood, and Stephen threw the bandage into the sink. He turned Parker's head and looked at the blood in his hair. He looked into his kit and pulled out a razor. "I'm going to have to shave your head to get down to the wound. I can't really see it with your hair in the way. It's covered in blood."

Normally, Parker would make a joke about having to shave his hair, but this wasn't normal. And he couldn't imagine ever being normal

225

again after what he had just seen. He didn't answer.

Stephen started to swipe away the hair that surrounded the wound. He used the sink to get the razor wet and worked his way delicately around it. "Can you give me some insight as to what happened? This is a pretty big head wound. Were you knocked out?"

Parker opened his mouth. "Yeah. I was hit from behind. I don't remember much after that, except when I woke up, this bandage was already on my head."

"You've got some blood on your forehead that doesn't correspond with any of the other wounds I'm finding on you. That's somebody else's blood, huh?" He asked slowly, and quietly.

Parker just made a small noise to confirm.

"You want to tell me why we're in a Super 8 outside of Chicago and not in a hospital? How did you even get here, Parker? Seriously. I'm not judging you. I'm here to help you. I've just flown all this way, I'm not here to judge."

He sighed. "I just... I've been through a lot recently, Stephen. I can't even believe I'm alive right now."

"Does this have anything to do with... your novel?" He asked.

226

Parker flinched as he felt a sharp pain from his head.

"Sorry." He reached into the kit and grabbed a small tube. "This is the glue they use in the ER for stitches, instead of threading. It won't hurt, I just want to make sure this gash is going to heal up without an infection. I'm glad whoever did this to you was gracious enough to clot the bleeding with the gauze, but they didn't bother cleaning it up first. Now, back to what I was saying. Your novel?"

Parker took a moment. "Yeah," he said. "How did you know?"

"You were acting different at Christmas. I know you. It wasn't you. I knew something was up, I just didn't realize it was this serious."

"I, uhh..." He hesitated.

Stephen finished up the wound dressing and rewrapped it with fresh gauze before backing away from the toilet he sat on. He looked at his brother.

Parker put his face in his hands as he felt heat rise to his cheeks. "I saw a man kill somebody and then commit suicide." He forced himself to say the words, and as he said them aloud, the scene flashed before his eyes.

"Shit," Stephen breathed. "Have you called the cops?" he asked, but his calmness kept

Parker calm, too. He appreciated it. "Have you involved authorities at all?"

Parker didn't answer.

"I'm judging by the fact we're in a dirty Super 8 motel bathroom that the answer is no..." He concluded.

The corner of Parker's mouth twitched. He wanted to laugh, but it didn't feel right. Didn't feel logical. "The man who did it was a bad guy. He hurt a lot of people in his lifetime. He's the man who was after me because I got involved with some important individuals when I published my novel. The man who did it was very powerful, if you know what I mean. He had connections everywhere. Including within the police. We couldn't get help."

Stephen nodded that he understood. "You gonna come home?"

Parker hesitated for another moment. "I'd like to. I have some things I need to take care of first... and I know I was just in Paris, but I really want to see Nori. Her parents helped me out when I needed it, before I was taken. And hopefully she's told them I'm alright now, but..."

Stephen nodded, then grabbed Parker's arm and examined his black and blue wrists, and the crease in his arm where the IV had bruised up.

"But I'll find my way home, eventually," he finished.

"How are things going with Nori?" Stephen asked.

"She's amazing. I think I love her. And not just some smitten love or something I would say to get into her pants... I mean I really, truly care for her."

Stephen smiled, "Good. Thanks for calling me, man. I'm glad you are *physically* all right. Just give yourself some time to heal. Don't move too fast. Mentally too."

He nodded. "I can't thank you enough," he said quietly. "I think I'm going to take a shower."

Stephen stood up from the ground and peeled off his gloves, tossing them into the trash and then washing his hands in the sink. "Yeah okay. Just don't get your head wet. Your face is okay, but I just changed the dressing around your head, so keep it back from the water."

"Okay. Thanks." He still just wasn't in the mood for jokes, which was what he'd normally do when somebody said a statement like that to him.

Stephen left the bathroom and closed the door behind him.

Parker heard him talking with Greysen and Molly as he leaned into the shower and turned on the facet. He felt the water until it turned from cold, to luke-warm, to hot. He peeled off his clothes as the steam rose up and out of the shower, fogging up the glass of the mirror.

He stepped inside, and his first thought was of all the feet that had stepped in this shower. Really, how clean was it? But none of that mattered after what had happened to him in the Humavision building, he supposed. He would never be the same again.

He was just a boring hipster from Kansas City who couldn't keep a day job. Regardless of what had happened in the last few days. His whole life had changed when he'd made the decision to drop everything and go to Paris. He'd thought about it over and over again.

Why had this happened to him? Sure, it'd been careless and risky for him to drop everything like that, but he was still young, and he'd had nothing tying him down. If he hadn't of gone, he wouldn't have been pursued by Greysen, who wouldn't have led him to Noriana. He wouldn't have written the novel that had become a bestselling thriller that had gotten him TV interviews. And if he hadn't of written that novel, he never would have been tracked down by Edrick and Molly.

Rusty brown water swirled around the drain. Some of that blood was his, and some of it wasn't. He released an audible sigh as he closed his eyes and put his face in the steaming water.

But why had Edrick gone through all of the trouble to find him and hurt him and steal his memories in hopes of tracking down Greysen, if he was just going to kill himself, anyway? Why would he give him that satisfaction? Why would he just give up like that? And it seemed like Allie had changed her mind about him in the end, no matter how mad she'd been with him. She's the one who had provided him the weapon.

Parker still just simply could not fathom what happened. It was going to take quite a bit of time to process all of it.

He allowed the water to flow over his sore body. He was grateful for his brother. A lot of his upbringing had been in the shadow of his perfect brother, while he was the clumsy one. They didn't have such a great relationship because of the age gap, and the fact that Parker felt like he was always being compared to Stephen's success. But Stephen wasn't half bad. He'd always been there when he needed him.

He thought about Noriana again and ached to see her. He leaned forward and turned the water off, stepping out of the shower and drying himself off with a towel. Because he didn't have an extra pair of clothes, he was going to have to put his stained, stiff clothing back on.

He finished getting dressed and opened the door to the main room.

Stephen was gone. Greysen and Molly sat in the bed together talking.

Parker made his way over to the little table. Just as he was about to sit, somebody knocked on the door to the motel room.

He looked up at the two. "Expecting someone?"

Greysen shook his head. "Maybe Stephen forgot something? Answer with caution," he said quietly as Parker walked towards the door.

Parker looked through the peephole. His body tensed up. "It's the cops!" he mouthed back to him, who moved to the edge of the bed at attention, his eyes wide.

"We have nowhere to run," Greysen said quietly.

Parker's heart thumped in his chest. Did Stephen call the police? *No... he wouldn't do that.* He reached forward and grabbed the knob, pulling the door towards him.

"Parker Rubec?" The policeman seemed surprised he had answered the door.

He nodded. "What can I do for you, officer?" *No need to panic here. It wasn't worth it.* So many thoughts were going through his mind. Why were the police here? Were they called in? How did they find them here and associate them back to the crime? Were they framed for Edrick's death? Was there more to the story than just a suicide?

The officer looked him up and down, clearly observing the bandage around his head. "I'm Officer Bradley. You must be Greysen Price, then?" he asked as he peered into the room.

Greysen stood up from the bed at attention.

The policeman backed up from the door and placed his hand on his hip.

Greysen raised his hands in the air. "I'm not going to pull anything," he said quietly.

"Why would you?" the officer asked pointedly.

"What do you want us to do, sir?" He asked.

Officer Bradley was quiet a moment. "I need to bring you all down to the station."

"No, c'mon," he protested. "Just take me. The kid didn't do anything wrong. He was just there."

"Exactly. He was there. We need to know exactly what's happened. People are dead here. We have reason to believe you two are innocent. But we need to take you in, anyway. Too much to explain right here."

Greysen looked back at Molly. "She's not fit to move," he said hopefully.

"I can have an ambulance come and pick her up," the officer said.

"No, that's not necessary," Molly chimed in from her place on the bed. "But it'd be nice to have a ride. I want to go with them to the station."

"No, Molls, I think it's better if you don't come," Greysen said.

"No, she's coming. If she refuses an ambulance, then my partner will take her." Officer Bradley motioned his head outside, where another cop car sat quietly next to his in the lot.

"Why can't Parker stay here with her?" Greysen asked.

The man shook his head. "No. You all need to come with us."

Parker and Greysen looked at each other. Greysen raised his eyebrow.

Parker wasn't entirely sure where all this was going, but apart from being in the room of the crime, he did nothing wrong. So, he focused on his breathing to stay calm as he followed Officer Bradley to his police car.

Greysen followed behind.

Officer Bradley opened the back door for them. "Obviously I'm not going to cuff you, but you have to sit in back. Okay?"

Parker slid into the car first, with Greysen behind him. He had seen the inside of the back of a police car far too many times in his life recently.

Greysen looked back to the motel room. "Molly?"

"My partner is going to escort her to the station. No need to worry." Officer Bradley shut the door and rounded the car to the driver's side. "Why didn't you come into the station right away, Greysen?" he asked as he got into the driver's seat and radioed in that he had picked them both up and they were on their way.

"C'mon now, Bill. You know I wouldn't. It's been such a long time. And... I don't know what story you guys have."

Parker looked back and forth between the officer and Greysen. "Wait... you know each other?" he asked, flabbergasted. "Why didn't you tell me?"

Greysen looked back over at him and nodded.

"I have no idea where the hell you've been hiding," Bill said, "but we do have a story, all right. And we need to hear yours, too. Especially because of the scene our boys walked in on at the Humavision headquarters."

Greysen's shoulders slumped forward.

235

Parker felt Greysen's body rise and fall in a hefty sigh next to him. He leaned his head against the window.

The drive to the station was long and grueling. Every single bump in the road made Parker's heart unexpectedly leap. If Greysen wanted to escape the grasp of the police, he could have. It was almost like he chose to get caught. Perhaps he was sick of running. Perhaps because of Edrick's life ending, he felt like he could be free. He didn't want to run anymore.

This was it. This is what life had handed to him.

TWENTY-FIVE

Greysen

Greysen watched a woman cop escort Parker into a holding room for questioning. He caught a glimpse of his face before the door closed. The kid looked defeated. Did he regret getting involved? Guilt swirled inside the pit of his stomach. It sickened him to think that he was the cause of so much pain for Parker physically, emotionally, and psychologically.

Ah... the kid will be okay. He heaved a sigh. *He's proven resilient.* The thought didn't make him feel any better. He tore his eyes away from the closed door of the holding room and turned to follow Bill into his office.

They weren't alone in there.

Bill took his seat behind his desk, lined with police awards. A white-haired man sat behind the desk as well.

Greysen moved towards one of the armchairs directly in front of the desk. He glanced over his shoulder at another officer in the room, who sat in a fold-out chair with his arms crossed. He looked back and forth a moment, and then took a seat in one of the armchairs.

"We are fairly certain," Bill began, "from the look of the room and the two people that remained there, about what happened there. It was a murder-suicide. But I brought you here because there was a special set of instructions I was supposed to relay to you, Greysen Price, in the event of Edrick Crowder's death." He reached forward and picked up a stack of papers from his desk.

Greysen readjusted himself to the edge of the chair, and hung onto his every word. "Wait, there were only two people in the room when you got there?" he interjected.

Bill nodded his head once, closing his eyes.

Peyton must have woken and taken off. Or somebody got to the room before them. He pushed the thought away for now. He needed to focus. "Why are you supposed to relay information to me? Of all people?" he asked.

"Greysen. Brace yourself. Edrick Crowder has written in his Last Will and Testament that in the event something happened to him, *you* were to inherent the company of Humavision, Inc. and all of its operations."

Greysen's throat instantly became dry. "Pardon?" he choked. He couldn't believe what he was hearing.

"The company is yours," Bill repeated.

"That bastard..." He breathed. He stood. "Why in the hell...?" His thoughts raced. Edrick had known he wanted nothing to do with that company. And then, for his last wish, to allow the company to come pouring down on his head... Edrick wanted him to have the thing he wanted to be far away from the most. Even in death, his ex-boss was still coming back to haunt him.

What was he to do with Humavision, of all things?

I could do what I'd intended to from the beginning...

I could repair what it has become...

That would require a lot of work.

"You can contact a lawyer if you'd like," Bill said. "But I thought I'd bring you down here myself to tell you."

"Well thanks, Bill. It's been... it's been quite an ordeal." He looked down around the legs of the armchair, as though magically a briefcase and his belongings would appear. Only, he had no belongings.

239

They shared a moment of silence as vent kicked on it the room.

"Where did you go, Greysen? We had an entire department dedicated to tracking you down for years after you were reported to have kidnapped his daughter."

"Those were lies," he snapped, and swiped his hand over his hair.

"Well, we are well aware of that now. Mrs. Crowder, nice woman, came to the station and cleared you of all charges. We didn't realize the custody battle mess that situation was. Regardless, I'm not sure what you were doing with the little girl in the first place."

His heart warmed at the mention of Corin's grandma. She had been sweet to him. Greysen hadn't thought of her in a long time. Though just as the memory was sweet and comforting, it also brought heartache. "The conditions were horrible for her. I was trying to help, to relocate her to one of her other relatives."

"You should have called child services."

He was quiet a moment. "But I didn't. Can't go back now. Would it be alright if I go? I... I have a lot of information to process... And I'd like to check on my friend." He looked back to the door. Suddenly, his shoulders felt heavy with the weight of the information he'd just received.

Humavision is... mine?

TWENTY-SIX

Parker sat in the hardback chair that reminded him of school while the police officers talked amongst themselves before turning to him for questions. At least he wasn't being treated like a criminal. They treated him as if he were helping them figure out the mystery.

But he wasn't sure he wanted them to know all the details of the events that took place in the Humavision building.

"How did you end up here, in Chicago?" The woman cop asked him as she sat behind the table that separated the two of them.

He reached up and scratched an itch that emerged just underneath his head bandage. "Uhh, it's hard for me to remember. I was staying at my girlfriend's family's vacation cabin about three hours outside of San Francisco, and they came as unexpected guests. The cabin is so far out in the middle of nowhere. And the last thing I remember is them knocking me out. From behind."

"Do you have any idea why they would come after you?" The woman police officer with her slicked black hair watched him carefully.

He shook his head, then looked down in his lap.

The other cop in the room listened quietly, scrawling notes in a small notepad, even when Parker hadn't talked.

The woman officer leaned forward over the table. "We found a gun with your fingerprints all over it near the scene of the crime. This gun." She took a gun inside an evidence bag, out from a drawer in the table, and placed it on top.

He raised his eyebrows. "Wow. You have— that's... wow. That's my girlfriend's dad's gun. I was staying up at the cabin alone, so he showed me where he kept it. If needed for self-defense. Sometimes bears and things are in the woods. So when I heard banging at the door of the cabin I ran and got his gun. Of course, it didn't do me any good. But they must have taken it. Would it be all right if I got that back? To return it to him?"

"Well it's being held as evidence right now, but if it turns out as irrelevant to the crime, we'll release it directly back to your girlfriend's father.

We'll be able to get his information from the serial number."

"Thank you. I appreciate that." He reached up and rubbed the back of his neck. "I'm not quite sure why I'm still here... in Chicago. I'd like to leave as soon as possible. Go back to my family in Kansas City. And let my girlfriend know I'm okay. Her parents were supposed to come back to the cabin and pick me up in five days and her father must have panicked when he saw the state of the cabin and the fact that I wasn't there."

"He still doesn't know what's happened?" she asked, and raised an eyebrow at him, then looked over to the other officer.

"Well I'm sure Noriana, my girlfriend, told him I'm alright. I've talked to her briefly."

"Why didn't we get any reports about this? I feel like if it was that serious, he would have at least contacted the San Francisco PD."

"Yeah, I told him to not contact anybody from the police department."

They stared blankly at him.

"Look." He sighed and moved his hands from his lap, to face down on the table between them. *Why are you holding back? They're here to help. You did nothing wrong.* "I knew that Edrick and his men were going to come for me. I wrote the book *The Idea man* for Greysen, about his life. And you all know that he disappeared. Those people wanted him. And they thought I had contact with him, which I didn't. At that point, I'd only met Greysen a few times. I mean, we spent time together, but it's not like I knew where he was after that time in Paris. That's where my involvement comes in here." Here he went again, telling complete strangers his whole life story. Except hopefully this time it was in his favor, and not against him. He wondered what was happening with Greysen and how his conversation was going in the other room.

"Alright, Parker. Thank you for speaking with us. Sit tight here for us to document some things and we'll be back for you."

The two cops rose from their seats and left the room.

He nodded. "Thanks," he mumbled as he looked down at the table. *How many other people have sat in this chair?*

With his back to the door, he laid his head down on the table while he waited for them to come back. He sighed, hoping it was sooner rather than later.

The door creaked open.

"You okay?" Greysen asked from behind.

Parker lifted his head. "Yeah, man. Just tired. What happened? Everything go okay for you?"

The look in his eyes made him appear ten times older. "He left me the entire company."

Parker stood. "Huh?"

"Edrick. He left me Humavision Inc. in his will. That's what they wanted me to know." He raised his hands and shrugged his shoulders.

"You're shitting me. Why'd he do that?" Parker furrowed his brow. He swiped an itch under his nose.

"I think it's because he wanted to give me the one thing I hated the most. And now I'm stuck leading these people, people who are relying on me for a job."

"Do you want to do it? Step up? Even if you hate it?"

"I don't know right now... it's insane how quickly plans can change." Greysen paced.

"Well, it sounds like you have a lot to think about," Parker concluded. "I just want to go home, really."

Just then, a police officer walked in and told them they were free to go.

They walked out of the police station, and Parker turned to Greysen.

"Hey man, I'm gonna go home. Back to Kansas City," he said.

Greysen nodded. "I wouldn't expect you to do anything less, and not in a bad way. I just mean, you've been through a lot that you weren't expecting to ever happen. And I just wanted to thank you for coming into my life. You have helped me in ways no other person ever has. Honestly. You helped me transcribe my story. Validated me."

Parker touched his hand up to his chest. His eyes were welling up, and he wasn't sure why he was so overcome with emotion. "I'll see you again someday, okay? Maybe in a happier setting. I need time to heal, I think."

Greysen nodded, and stuffed his hands in his pockets. He sniffled. "Let me go back in and call you a cab to take you to O'Hare, the airport."

"Thanks." He clasped his hand on Greysen's shoulder before the older man turned and walked back into the police station.

He bounced up and down on his heels, the bitterness of the January Chicago wind biting his neck, but he didn't care. He was going to have to move on in his life, having seen all the things he had. He was ready to bunker down and live a boring, stress-free life in the River Market of Kansas City. And even though he was a writer, he wanted to sit and not have any external material to influence his work. Perhaps he might even take a break from writing all together. Maybe find a job and work a repetitive pattern until he was ready to move on again.

Who am I kidding? His girlfriend was in Paris, and he had nothing for him back in Kansas City besides a mediocre past, and his family, of course... who were all busy with their own lives. He'd finally made something of himself, helping Greysen with this story, even if it had been by accident. He'd had courage and bravery to live out a real-life action film, and he was not the victim.

He was the hero of the story. The hero who was brought into this mess by being in the wrong spot at the wrong time—just like how Spiderman started out.

I am like Spiderman. He smirked as Greysen came back out onto the front sidewalk of the police station.

"What are you smiling about?" He asked, wearing a smirk himself.

Parker shook out of his trance. "I dunno. I'm just grateful to be alive I guess," he answered quietly. "What are you going to do after I leave? Are you and Molly okay?"

He shook his head, his smile fading underneath the long, greying beard. "No. She's not... I don't know. She wants to take it slow and that's understandable. She's feeling guilty about something she's done. Probably a lot of things she's done, really, and I think she feels like she doesn't deserve me, maybe?"

"But you don't care about any of that," He interjected.

"Exactly. I told her we could start over, but she still seemed hesitant. I mean, I understand if she doesn't..." his voice croaked, "...have those strong feelings about me anymore. But if she doesn't want to be with me because of past things she's done, I don't really get that."

"Girls are complicated, man," Parker said, thinking about Noriana. "And if Molly is feeling the way I do after having gone through what we just did—even though she was knocked out for the part I keep replaying again and again in my head, then she's really going to need some space for a minute."

The two guys stood quietly together, while different cars passed in the street in front of the police building.

"It's only human for you to do that, you know. Replay it over and over. That's normal, Parker. I'm sorry you had to see and go through that." He looked to the ground.

Parker shrugged. "At least that wasn't us in the end. At least we are standing here having this conversation together."

Just then, the burnt yellow cab pulled up in front of the station.

"What are you going to do about Humavision?" Parker asked as he reached for the door handle.

"I... I don't know. I think a lot of people are relying on a leader, so they can keep their jobs and provide for their families." He turned away from him.

"Oh my God, you're going to do it. Aren't you?" Parker asked, more in a curious tone than an accusing one.

"I can invent any kind of company I want to. See, Edrick thinks he's left me a burden, but I now see an opportunity."

He smiled and then nodded back. "I'm not sure what you wanted to end up happening here, and it probably worked in your favor because you weren't the one that had to end it, but perhaps you can continue to get your revenge while he's in the grave."

The cab driver honked, and Parker jumped. He opened the door. "Hang on a minute, man!" He then turned back to Greysen. "But also make sure to be careful and watch your back. You don't know what kind of traps he's planted, people or operations-wise. You don't know if there's a bigger picture here other than him leaving you a company in his will."

Greysen nodded at him. "Trust me, I know. Don't worry. I'll be keeping an eye out, that's for sure. You take care. Call me if you need anything. And Parker, if you ever find yourself needing a job, I'm sure we could find some need for a writer here."

He smiled. "Thank you, Greysen. You take care, too." Then he ducked into the back seat of the cab and slammed the door.

The driver took off before he could even get his seat belt buckled in.

"O'Hare, please," He called to the front.

"O'Hare? You don't need me to take you to a halfway house or somethin'? What are you, just out on bail?"

He stifled a laugh. "You don't know the least of it."

The cabbie grunted in response, but to Parker's relief, didn't continue that conversation thread. The rest of the cab drive passed in silence.

He felt foreign in his own skin. Everything that had happened to him in the previous days was so out of his comfort zone that he felt disconnected from his everyday life back in Kansas City.

Much like he often felt when traveling, branching out and not familiar with a particular place because the language was different, the laws were different, the way the people carried themselves was different, and it would always make him feel further and further away from his home. Like his roots were ripped up from the ground and he was made to live in his strange skin.

However, every time he came home from traveling and got back into his normal, same routine, he would look back and miss it. He would realize, once removed from the situation, that he'd actually learned a lot about a new culture, and more importantly, about himself.

He'd grown.

The only thing that comforted him now, sitting in the back of that awkward, smelly cab all the way to the airport in Chicago, was the simple fact that maybe, just maybe, once he was settled back home and began to once again feel even just the slightest sense of normalcy, maybe he would grow from this. Maybe he would learn something new about himself that would help him to become a better person at the end of all of this.

Maybe he would miss these times.
But only time would tell.

TWENTY-SEVEN

Greysen

Greysen sat behind a card table with a fold-out chair.

It was an office on the second floor. Not the old CEO's office. He couldn't fathom setting up his space in the same place that Edrick had used as his headquarters. Even though it was in a convenient, central location, the things that had happened in that office were memories he wanted to forget. He also couldn't go back to his small closet office on the first floor. It had been repurposed as a janitorial closet after it was destroyed, anyway, but besides that, too many memories were there as well.

If he was going to run this company, he had to start fresh.

Am I even cut out to run this company? A small part of him felt on the cusp of learning what it really took to run a company like this, and he wasn't sure he had the tools inside him to achieve that goal.

There was something that just wasn't right about the whole situation. Why had the man who had been trying to find him and kill him for several years past, end up giving him the company? And what had driven Edrick to such a brutal end? Perhaps he was sick of chasing, just as much as Greysen was sick of running. Or perhaps the company had driven him to do such a thing because of the pressure and nature of his work.

He *had* used the memory invention on Edrick, after all. It was obvious there were things he'd done in his past that maybe nobody else had known about, and an invasion of privacy was enough to uncover those memories. Maybe he hadn't been able to bear the thought of others finding out about those things.

Regardless, he was gone. And Greysen had to look forward.

Since he had taken the job as President and CEO of Humavision Inc, he had moved back to Chicago, into a small duplex. He'd shaved his overgrown beard and got a haircut, of course, so that his appearance looked clean-shaven.

Every day he thought of his experience living in France. It helped him to live his life completely different from before. Even though he was considerably one of the richest men in Chicago now, he still chose to live modestly. He still lived in that small duplex and took public transportation. And every time he would step off the L, he would always acknowledge the pan handlers and homeless sitting with their change cups and instrument cases. He would always give them everything that was in his pockets at the time. It was the least he could do.

He'd planned a meeting with the executives of the company the week following his takeover of Humavision. Whispers were shared around the building.

A new CEO.

Edrick was gone.

And this new CEO had a different direction for the company.

The rest of what was passed around was unclear.

To his knowledge, nobody knew the details or events as to why Edrick was no longer their leader, nor had they heard who was going to take his place.

As he sat there thinking of all the things that had happened in the recent days, and everything he'd need to get together for the days to come, he thought about his Memory Machine. It had been prematurely created from blueprints he had invented years ago. He'd chosen not to actually create the invention because there were just too many unpredictable variables that came along with it. His vision was to create an invention that would be able to help people. To make the lives of people easier, and to help them in any way he could. And even though this memory machine needed a lot of tweaking, it had still been neat to see it in use.

He had a computer on the desk in front of him that he could not access. He'd tried for days. He'd used to be great at hacking software, but he must have been rusty from all his years of lying dormant. This one he just could not break.

The password to the secure servers he needed access to for information regarding how to run the company's day-to day-protocol was only known by one person: Edrick Crowder.

Greysen propped his elbows on the desk and rested his face in his hands. Of course, Edrick wasn't going to make this easy. Why would he? Not only did he leave the responsibility of the thing he hated the most in his hands, but he also wasn't going to make it a piece of cake to takeover. What was he getting at? *Did he want me to fail? Be responsible for the loss of all these employees' jobs? Show me what would have happened years ago, had I succeeded in destroying Humavision?*

He pushed back in the chair and stood, walking over to the window that overlooked the street below.

The thought of Edrick wanting him to fail, irked him. But he couldn't let it get to him. And he couldn't fail.

Of course, there was always the memory chip.

He shifted from one foot to the other, then crossed his arms. He could have access to all the information he needed. Only he hadn't made the decision to watch the chip yet, yet because of what he'd promised to Molly. He'd kept the memories locked away. But it taunted him. The whole reason they'd hooked his ex-boss up to that machine was, not only to give him a taste of his own medicine and slice open his privacy, but also for proof of his character. Of everything he'd done.

Only he hadn't realized the repercussions that would have on the good guys too.

On Molly.

Greysen's gaze followed a woman on the sidewalk below, a to-go coffee cup in hand. She flagged down a cab.

Molly had been keeping her distance. She seemed to just be busy all the time. When he'd see her in the hallways, she'd distantly smile at him and continue on her way. He didn't try very often, but she would never answer her phone, either. He wanted to give her the space she needed, though, so he stayed clear.

And he supposed he was used to being without her, anyway, from so many years of grieving because he thought she'd been killed.

He sighed and rubbed his hands over his face. It felt as though, despite their shared love many years ago, after all this distance apart, they were simply just two different people.

Even still, he'd told her he wouldn't watch Edrick's memories because the thought of it had overwhelmed and upset her. He'd told her they could start their relationship over from the beginning, with no judging or using their pasts against each other.

But now... now he was faced with the problem of needing information about Humavision he couldn't get otherwise, due to Edrick's untimely death. He needed to watch those memories in order to run this company.

People were counting on him to keep this place afloat. He had no choice. *Right?*

He looked away from the window, to the door of his office. He needed to hook himself up to his own invention.

TWENTY-EIGHT

Greysen

A soft knock sounded at the door of the lab. Greysen had gotten down there first, and he opened it to let Carrie in, a young, dark-haired girl with pale white skin. She was one of Humavision's research and innovators, and she was currently helping him to redevelop the memory invention with a different blue-print and prototype.

"I told you that you weren't going to be able to do it on your own," she smirked, closing the door and locking it.

"Well, I can handle the machine, but I need somebody to monitor my vitals as I'm in sleep mode," he uttered in a hushed tone.

"I can do that." She took her place at the computer.

He eased up onto the bed that was slightly reclined, so he could sit upright. This time around,

263

there were no restraints. He took his suit jacket off and hung it over the chair that sat next to the bed. Then, he unbuttoned his collared shirt just enough to place the pulse meters on his chest in various places. His hand trembled as he secured the electrode sticky dots, nerves pumping through his body. Nerves… *and guilt*. But he was here. He was in too deep. He needed to venture into Edrick's mind for the advantage, no matter the cost at this point. At least that's what he'd told himself.

Carrie moved from the computer to help, rolling his left shirt sleeve up to reveal the underside of his elbow. "You want me to do it or are you good?" she asked, her eyebrow raised.

"I'll do it," he said quietly, taking the needle from her.

She wrapped a tourniquet around his bicep and tied it tight, revealing his bulged veins.

He inserted the needle, biting his lip as he watched himself break his own skin.

Carrie watched a moment, then screwed on the tube that led up to the yellowish liquid that would send him into dream world. The process was similar to extracting the memories, only in reverse. In order to retrieve someone else's memories, their extracted memories chip was inserted into the system. The person retrieving the data, Greysen in this case, would not only watch, but fully immerse himself inside Edrick's memories. To him, they would feel like a dream that he was a spectator inside.

Right after Carrie connected the serum, she sat back and hovered her hand over the computer. "This is the chip here, right?"

He nodded, looking over at the chip on the cart next to the computer. Carrie picked it up with her gloved hand, as though it were a delicate entity.

"Yeah." He laid his head back. "I'll see you in a little bit. Just... don't let anybody come through the door. And, whatever you do... whatever reaction I have, Carrie, do not wake me up. Okay? I'm going to be experiencing some pretty intense things, but just leave me until it's finished."

She nodded. "Okay, boss. As long as you are physically all right, I won't terminate it," she promised.

He let out a sigh of relief and leaned back onto the table. "Thanks, Carrie. I'm ready."

Greysen was numb. Dizzy. He swirled in a drunk, sleepy state. Pictures flashed across his vision like a dream. One flaw of the invention that hadn't been quite worked out yet was the inability to sift through the memories to only the specific ones he wanted. His thoughts underneath had the influence to hone in on a focus, but it was highly touchy.

He didn't feel the sense of invading somebody's privacy this time at least, like he'd imagined he would when he created the invention, because the person he was infiltrating was dead. That made it a little bit easier.

The first memory his mind landed on caught his eye because he recognized the small child standing there. Corin was younger than when he'd first met her back in the mansion years ago. A woman stood at the doorstep with the terrified child and presented her to Edrick.

Greysen's body flooded with anxiousness and hatred toward the little girl in front of him. That little girl had done nothing to deserve this. Underneath the feelings, he felt repulsed for having even felt this. But these weren't his emotions. These were the emotions of Edrick at the time of this memory, bogging down his own.

His perspective wasn't from *inside* Edrick's body. He was more like a shadow.

The woman at the door wore a social services lanyard. She explained it'd taken them a while to get a hold of him, and that they'd been trying to reach him ever since the passing of the girl's mom.

266

Greysen had had no idea that Corin's mother had passed away. That must have been why she'd needed to come to America to live with Edrick. He had never contemplated what had happened between Corin's mother and Edrick, though he also never understood why he had ended up with Corin in his care.

If he dove deeper into this pot of memories, surely he'd be able to find out that as well. But that wasn't why he was here. He just needed the codes to operate Humavision. That's all. He had to keep his goal in mind, hoping that maybe, just maybe, the machine was smart enough to be influenced by his intentions.

As he watched other pictures flash before his eyes, another thought occurred to him. What if Edrick had purposefully not included the passcodes in his will, not because he wanted Greysen to be responsible for the collapse of the company... but because he *wanted* him to look back at his memories?

What if Edrick had *wanted* him to see what Molly had done? He panicked.

And as if by magic, just when he thought Molly's name, her face appeared in the next memory. He was brought back to one of the worst days of his life, though now he saw it through Edrick's perspective.

He sat in the office of one of his employees, whom he'd kicked out moments before. Why couldn't he be in his own office? Because his office was occupied. Because the scene where Molly was tased in Edrick's office by Dolor and Price was about to happen.

How they'd gotten through the building with her body and nobody else seeing them, Greysen still didn't understand. That was something he'd have to be sure couldn't happen at Humavision on his watch. No more shady dealings, no more physical violence against its own employees... none of that would have a place at Humavision any longer.

Edrick sat, tapping his shoe on the ground impatiently, until the office door was kicked in and they brought Molly in, dropping her on the floor.

Greysen felt his muscles constrict, and he couldn't tell if it was in his head, or if he was also making these movements in real life for Carrie to see.

He remembered the security video feed of them shocking Molly with the taser because they hadn't liked something she said, and then dragging her out of the room by her hair after she'd been left unconscious. At the time, he couldn't hear what their conversation was about because the security videos didn't have sound.

All these years, he'd assumed it was because they had found out about his and Molly's intimate relationship. Though if that were the case, why not just fire one or the other? Why take it to these kinds of measures?

Now... now he was about to find out what had really been said.

He struggled with this reality. He had a fleeting moment of his heartrate picking up. Surely if he kept this up, Carrie would pull him back out. But then... an emotion much stronger than guilt emerged. *Curiosity.* Was there anything Molly could do or say that would make him think differently of her? Surely, there would be an explanation for it, if so.

He swallowed hard and stayed in the memory of that office, with Edrick sitting on top of the desk and Molly laying on the ground before him. When she stirred, Greysen's heart leapt. She moaned on the floor and picked herself up, glancing sideways at Edrick.

"Fuck you," she breathed through her lips, the drool dripping off and onto the floor.

He felt a sickly joy in his gut. *Edrick's emotions.*

"It's all part of the bigger picture, sweetheart," Edrick said to her. "You knew about this before you got involved with him."

Greysen struggled to keep up.

"I didn't know that would happen," she whispered with a rasp, looking down and wiping her mouth. "I want out. I really do like him, Ed. Please. Please just let me out."

He watched her face screw up and her eyes fill with tears. He wanted to bend down and hold her, to comfort her. *Ed? Why's she calling him Ed?*

"You know too much, Molly." Edrick's voice was much lower now. "It's too late for you to be *out*. You chose this."

"None of us chose this," she spat back.

He was quiet a moment.

Greysen furrowed his brow. *What the hell are they talking about?* Apparently so much more was going on behind the scenes than he'd ever imagined. It didn't seem Molly wanted to be there, and he liked to think she had been forced to work against him, not done it by choice.

But could she have been plotting against him and never told him what was really going on, despite all the time they spent together? He felt an ounce of betrayal, but that was quickly extinguished by his next thought: perhaps she had to do this to survive.

And she was a survivor. Just like him.

And he loved her.

"Sure, none of us chose this," Edrick said then. "And nothing has changed since then... we still don't have a choice. And you work for me," he continued. "If you try to pull anything suspicious—and trust me, I will have all eyes on you—then things will become very difficult for you from here on out."

Molly shot up a look of disgust as she tried to push herself to standing.

"Whoa whoa, I'd take your time. It's not so easy after all of your muscles have been forcefully contracted," he smirked, then stood up off the desk and worked his way around to the door. "Whenever you're ready, somebody will be waiting for you outside to escort you to your next project."

And just like that, he left the room and with Edrick, so did Greysen.

He wanted to stay behind and comfort her, but these were not his memories. All he could do was watch them unfold like a movie.

TWENTY-NINE

Greysen

*F*ind the codes.

His goal was to find the codes. None of this betrayal stuff or conspiring against him mattered anymore.

Edrick was dead.

Greysen was now head of Humavision, and he needed to discover how to access all the files that would help him be able to see into the heart and brain of this company, in order to run it correctly.

Years ago, he thought he'd destroyed Humavision when he'd destroyed their servers. It had been a major setback for them, sure, but in this day and age, mostly everything was digital. All the information was still out there in cyberspace.

As if he had any control over what memory of Edrick's he would experience next, his mind focused in on the thought of him sitting at his desk in his normal office. His face and body in the reflection of the computer monitor looked rough. He was beat. It looked like he probably should have been seen by a doctor or perhaps even have gone to the ER. Greysen recognized the goose egg on his head because it was from him. Edrick must have gone straight from his mansion, to work, to see that everything wasn't gone from the company. He was panicky, flinching, and looking up at every opportunity he got.

He felt a tiny bit of satisfaction for being the cause of Edrick's distress in this moment.

Edrick tapped into the computer, and Greysen was able to see what the password was as his stubby fingers punched the keyboard. He would make note of that in his head for later, so he could have access into the computer.

As the desktop unlocked, a blinking icon at the bottom was obnoxiously raving. Edrick painfully sighed as he clicked it. It was a webcam chat, and somebody was calling him right now.

The video feed filled his screen. The resolution was far blurrier than any technology they had now. The person on the other side stood back in shadow so their face was concealed. "What in the hell happened over there?" the voice asked, uncharacteristically calm for the cowardly reactions he was putting off.

"H-he knocked me out," He squeaked. "He destroyed all the servers in my mansion."

"You had one job."

"I know. I'm sorry."

"Cut the shit. You know what you need to do."

If Greysen was confused before, he had no idea *what* world he was in now. It appeared that Edrick was speaking to a higher-up.

He is not... the leader? He couldn't believe the connections this was making in his mind as it ran a billion miles a minute.

So Edrick was not the leader of this operation, like Greysen had been led to believe all these years. He was answering to a boss, himself.

And his boss was not happy with what he had done.

Then all of a sudden, everything began to make sense as to why he had committed suicide. He'd felt like he'd had no choice. He'd failed the mission he was set out to accomplish. He needed to prove to this higher up that he could take care of things. Find Greysen, and make him pay for what he did. In Edrick's mind, Greysen didn't know the least of it.

And judging by the emotions he felt as everything unraveled, he didn't.

Where it went wrong for Edrick, was when *he* was caught and hooked up to the memory machine. Before that, perhaps he saw a way of escaping and getting out, using him as an example.

Greysen had been able to hide out for so long undetected, with even the best spies searching high and low for him. Perhaps Edrick could do the same thing? And escape his chains. But when he'd finally found him, Greysen was fighting the wrong enemy. Edrick was not his enemy. He was only the face. The figurehead.

When Greysen caught him and strapped him to the memory machine, Edrick knew it was all over. He was going to have seen too much. And there was nothing left for him to do. So, he'd ended it. On his own terms instead of his boss's.

And that only meant one thing for Greysen.

Whoever this shadow man was... whoever was controlling Edrick's decisions for Humavision, whether they worked within the company, or was a side hustle, they were going to contact him. He would find out soon enough.

It was all just a matter of time.

The images meshed together, blending and blurring until his eyes fluttered open and he saw the white ceiling above him of the lab. Carrie stood over him, the tube from the IV in her hand. She'd unscrewed it. Her eyes were piercing.

"Wha—"

"Don't speak," she said quietly. "Take your time. Just allow yourself to come back out of it slowly. Regroup."

Greysen's heart pounded and raced, and his dampened skin told him he'd been sweating.

Carrie sat down in the chair next to the computer and typed into it before looking back over at him. "That bad, huh? Your vitals skyrocketed. To dangerous levels."

He blinked his eyes repeatedly to try and bring himself to. "It was... yeah. It was a lot," he said, feeling as if a major weight had dropped onto his chest.

Just when he'd thought it was over....

All of the relief he'd felt for the era of Edrick finally ending had now extinguished, because it seemed that man had been merely a small piece in the grand scheme of things.

Just when he'd thought it was over, it was only just beginning.

"This was a mistake..." he breathed.

"Well, at least now you know the truth," Carrie said optimistically. She had no idea what he'd just witnessed.

"No."

"It wasn't the truth?" she asked.

"No... looking at the memories wasn't the mistake..." He took his time formulating the words. "Coming back here, to Chicago, was a mistake."

She looked around the room and then back at him. "You don't want to run Humavision?" She furrowed her brow.

He shook his head. "I will... I will never be the one running this company."

"What do you mean, you're going to leave again?" she asked, a hint of panic and confusion in her voice. She looked down at his wrist. "This will pinch for a second." She peeled the tape off his skin and slipped the needle out, then closed a cotton ball over the hole and held pressure to it to clot it.

As she wrapped the tape over the cotton, he flinched. Though he'd been through worse. "No. I mean, I will never be the one in control. There will always be someone or something higher than me, dictating my every move." *At least Carrie didn't know anything about this...*

"Can't you change that? Turn everything around?" she asked hopefully.

He had to appreciate her optimism in a dark time. Her ignorance to the whole situation. "Thank you for helping me do this, Carrie. You've been a great coworker and friend."

She nodded, and turned back to cleaning their work up.

He didn't know what to do now. He moved his legs to the side of the bed and used the bed to aid himself in standing. His legs felt like Jell-O, but he could still walk.

He needed to board himself up in his office and think of his next move, before it was decided for him.

THIRTY

"Noriana Page," the woman called out.

Parker stood in the back of the auditorium and watched the beautiful, long-haired girl walk across the stage wearing her robes and a square hat with a tassel on the side. The smile that was painted across her red lips showed one of pride and accomplishment. Parker had one mirroring hers on his own face as well.

She shook hands with the University president and received her diploma, stopped for a photo, and then made her way back to her seat as the next graduate walked across the stage. He felt an overwhelming burst of pride for Noriana, finishing what she'd set out to finish, and even more excitement that he was able to be here to share it with her.

As the ceremonies came to an end, he waited in the lobby holding a bouquet of roses for her. As he watched all the same-colored robes emerge from the door, somebody touched him on the back of the shoulder. He spun around to see Jack and Anya standing there. Without thinking, he threw his arms around both of them, greeting them in the most unlikely Parker-way imaginable.

"It's so good to see you," Anya said gracefully as they hugged.

"I cannot... I cannot thank you guys enough," he said shakily, feeling emotion emerge behind his throat.

"I'm just happy to see you are alive, after the state of that cabin when I went back," Jack whispered, looking around to make sure nobody was listening in.

"I am happy to be alive, too," Parker laughed. "Turns out isolating myself as opposed to being around a lot of people in a public place wasn't the best way to hide from someone," he joked. He was slowly but surely beginning to feel more like himself these days. "Also, please let me pay for whatever was trashed in your cabin once I left. I, unfortunately, wasn't conscious to see the state it was left in." The memory was still fresh in his head.

Jack closed his eyes and brushed his hand away as if to gesture that it was no big deal. "Don't worry about it, kid."

Just when Parker was about to protest, Noriana came up to their circle.

"Oh, congratulations, sweetie!" Anya threw her arms around Noriana and while they hugged, Noriana winked at Parker.

He couldn't help but grin.

She went over and hugged her Dad as well, and then took out her cell phone. "Hey Parker, can you take a photo of us?"

"Of course." He took her phone and backed up as Jack and Anya stood on either side of Noriana with their arms around her.

"We are so proud of you," Jack said as they all smiled and Parker snapped a few photos of them on Noriana's cell phone. As soon as they were done, and her parents said a few more words of admiration to her, they left, allowing Noriana and Parker time to themselves.

He took her hand and Noriana led him into an elevator. When they were alone behind the closed automatic doors, Noriana leaped onto him.

He took her in his arms and kissed her harder than he'd ever kissed another human in his entire life.

"I'm so happy you could make it," she said excitedly, taking her place next to him as the door to the elevator opened. She led them out onto the roof of the Museum of Modern Art in San Francisco.

The rooftop overlooked the entirety of the skyline of downtown, with the bay sparkling behind it. As if anything else besides the woman holding his hand could take his breath away, his heart began to beat faster in his chest.

They walked up to the overhang of the building and looked over.

"So, what's next for you—for us?" he asked her, reaching over and putting a piece of her hair behind her ear.

"I ..." She seemed nervous.

"Alright. Lay it on me," he joked. He knew something was up.

"I took a job, Parker."

"Holy shit, that's amazing, Nori! Already? Your hard work has paid off!" He was genuinely excited for her, no matter what that meant for him.

She couldn't contain her own excitement and laughed in spite of her seeming nervousness. Instantly after, a sadness took the place of the elation on her face.

His smile faded as he stood there, both of her hands in his. "What's the job?"

"I'll be one of the junior curators for a museum. It's in France, Parker," she said quietly, placing her hand on his shoulder.

They stood a moment together, overlooking the city and hanging on to the rail as the San Franciscan wind swayed their bodies.

"How long does it take to get a visa?" he asked, looking forward.

"I already have... my visa," she said slowly.

He looked at her and smirked.

"Parker! I can't ask you to drop everything and go with me!"

"You're not asking me. I'm just going to do it."

She stood back from him, her hand reaching up to her mouth. "Are you serious?" She playfully hit his arm. "You can't be serious!"

He shrugged. "Nori. I'm a writer. I can make my life anywhere I want to. And anyway, I can fully say that Paris is where my life changed forever."

"Because it's when you became involved with all that stuff having to do with Greysen," she whispered.

"No," he said firmly. "I mean yes, all that stuff happened. But my life changed forever, because that is where I met you." His heart thumped.

She turned her head and looked at him, a small smile on her lips, and tears quivering at her lashes.

"My life would not be complete without you," he said, moving in for a kiss.

"Then let's go to Paris together," she whispered in-between kisses.

"I'm not sure how it's going to work out, but I do know that I need to get started on my next novel," he said, grinning sheepishly once more.

"Well, at least you'll have a lot of material to work with," she joked.

He smiled and nodded. To say the least, that was true.

Three Months Later...

Noriana wouldn't be home for a while, so Parker went out to do his favorite thing, which was to stand on the bridge outside of the Cathédrale Notre-Dame de Paris and watch the sun set underneath the Seine River. Hues of orange reflected off the romantic swells in the water. He couldn't think of anywhere else he wanted to make his home, with a person he loved. In the end of it all, he felt like he'd won.

Greysen had won, too, getting the company he deserved. And neither one of them needed to worry about running for their lives anymore.

As the sun sank lower under the fronts of the majestic and historical architecture of the buildings, Parker decided to make his way back home. The metro wasn't always his favorite place to be after dark. He waited at the street corner and went on the crosswalk when the green man on the signaler across the street appeared in the box. Just as he was passing in front of the Notre Dame, he saw a man with a long beard and wearing a large coat, lean over and pick up a piece of a sandwich wrapper, checking to see if anything was inside.

For a moment, Parker thought he caught a glimpse of the man's face. And it looked like a very familiar face.

His stomach did a somersault. "Could it be—" He thought of marching over there, grabbing the homeless man by his shoulder and turning him to get a better look at his face. But that wasn't logical, obviously.

Parker squeezed his eyes shut and opened them again, shaking his head to rid himself of the thought. "No, there's no way it could be him. He's all the way across the world right now." He scoffed at himself, then continued walking with his head down. He needed to get home before Noriana did, or else she'd be worried that he had gotten himself into some other kind of trouble, and trouble was the last place on Earth he wanted to be.

"That would make for a good story, though," he said to himself, and he laughed as he went down the ceramic stairs to the metro.

The End

WANT TO SEE WHAT HAPPENS NEXT?

www.kristinhelling.com/thetrueman

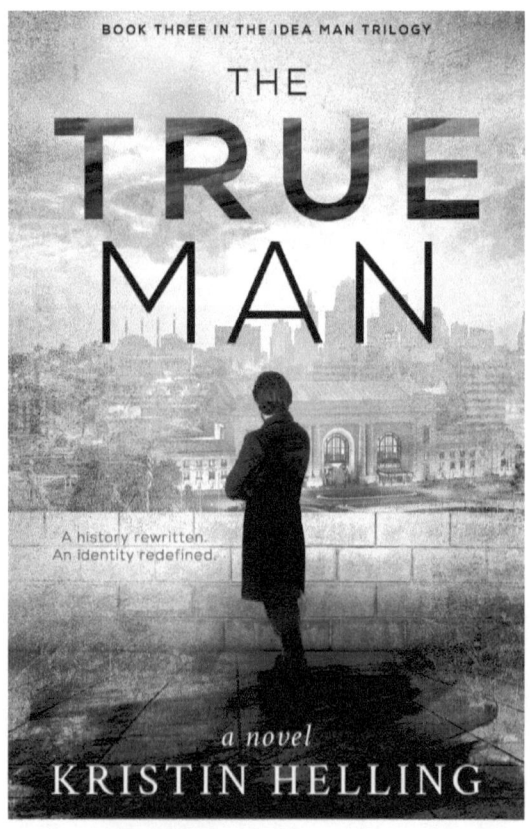

A history rewritten. An identity redefined.

Greysen Price now has the job he'd always wanted from the beginning. He recovered his recent memory invention with that, his power. Though as he's sifting through, he becomes lost. Are the memories playing as they happened, or as the person remembers them?

In addition to adjusting to his new rank, Greysen discovers that the boss he thought he eradicated, wasn't really the boss at all. And this new, bigger boss has games of his own.

Parker Rubec is living his new life in Paris, when he gets a call about his parents that crashes his whole world. He must return to Kansas City. He knows Greysen is pulling him back into a mess that could get him killed, but he reenters with a new confidence.

When Parker learns a new piece of information about his past, he questions the makeup of his whole identity, and if it's worth saving or redefining.

THE TRUE MAN is the 3rd and final book in The Idea Man Triology. If you enjoy a story with heart-pounding twists and turns around every corner, you will love the ending to this fast-paced thriller trilogy.

www.kristinhelling.com/thetrueman

A NOTE FROM
THE AUTHOR

Dear Reader,

Thank you for taking the time to read the continuation of Parker and Greysen's story.

If you've enjoyed this book, please help others find it by writing a review on Amazon or Goodreads. This is the number one best way to show an author you enjoyed their work.

And as always, thank you for being on this journey with me.

Kristin Helling

ABOUT THE AUTHOR

Kristin Helling enjoys stories with a journey—whether it's a journey across the globe, a journey through space, or a journey of finding one's self.

She writes primarily adult fiction thrillers. She's published a standalone Sci-fi thriller called *Capsule*, and a 4-book crime thriller series called the *Mastermind Murderers*. When she's not killing people (fictionally, of course!), she also has a passion for children's stories and writes them under the pen name Kristin Alis.

Kristin owns a coffee house in Kansas City MO, co-owns the publishing imprint Wordwraith Books, is married to a Photographer, and is Mama to one little boy and his hairy sibling, a collie-shepherd mix.

Find more books by Kristin Helling at
www.kristinhelling.com

Sign up for bonus content at
www.kristinhelling.com/jointhejourney

ALSO BY KRISTIN HELLING

Books available where all books are sold.

THE IDEA MAN TRILOGY
(comedic, suspense thriller)

The Idea Man
The Marked Man
The True Man

THE MASTERMIND MURDERERS SERIES
(psychological, crime thriller)

The Altruism Effect
The Bystander Effect
The Carbon Effect
The Domino Effect

STANDALONE SERIES
(soft sci fi Thriller)

Capsule